AN EMORY CRAWFORD MYSTERY NOVEL

The Devil's Hook

by Pearl R. Meaker

PROMONTORY
P R E S S

Promontory Press
www.promontorypress.com

ISBN: 978-1-987857-16-0

Cover design by Marla Thompson of Edge of Water Designs
Typeset by One Owl Creative in 13 pt Adobe Jenson Pro

Printed in Canada
0123456789

"Some commit murder,
some get mixed-up in murders,
others have murder thrust upon them.
My Aunt Jane comes into
the third category."

Raymond West
about Miss Marple
In
Greenshaw's Folly
By
Agatha Christie

The Devil's Hook

Chapter 1

"OKAY, EVERYONE. MONDAY WE LEARNED CROCHET TERMS AND abbreviations, chaining, and slip stitch to form a ring. Tuesday we learned single crochet both by counting stitches back from the hook and using our line of chain stitches as the base to build the single crochet stitches on and by making a ring and working the single crochet stitches into the ring. We also learned to make a double crochet stitch and we worked double crochet along a line of chain stitches and also worked them into a ring. Those two days gave you the basis of all crocheting. With those stitches and techniques you will be able to do a vast number of patterns and be set to learn other types of stitches as well. Today we will be starting the afghan shown on the pattern sheet in your packet."

I smiled and waved the pattern at the group of students sitting in a cozy semi-circle around the fireplace in our family room. Yes, students. Even though I only have a bachelor's degree ofttimes people with enough life experience in a field are allowed, by the accrediting agencies, to teach courses for credit.

"We have them, Mrs. Craw … Emory," piped up Carrie, an elfin blonde and a math whiz. A couple of students smiled and obligingly waved their copies back at me.

Except for Amy Twombly, who held hers up, pinched between her thumb and forefinger by one edge midway down the page, as though she didn't want to touch it. It flopped over like a dead fish.

"Okay, let's get out our hooks and whatever yarn you're wanting to start your project with and I'll start demonstrating the pattern. There's a bit of a trick to it that you'll need to see done, I think, in order to understand it. Once you learn it the rest is easy-peasy."

While everyone was busy getting set up, I thought about Amy.

On Monday, the first day of my January, or "J term," class, I always ask the students why they are taking my course, which is knitting one year and crochet the next. I usually get a set of rather stock answers:

"My grandma did this and I thought I'd like to learn."

"My girlfriend is here"—usually accompanied by a blush.

"My dorm room is cold and I decided I wanted an afghan."

But Amy's response was 100 percent pure Amy Twombly.

"I was skimming around online and somehow ended up somewhere that mentioned Vana White yarn. I thought, 'Wow, Vana does things with yarn?' I mean, even if all she does is walk back and forth and turn letter panels around, she is a celebrity. I've always thought it was … you know, knitting and crocheting were … ah … too old fashioned to be anything someone like me would be doing, but if Vana does yarn crafts it couldn't be too bad. She is lovely and stylish and I'm sure worth millions. So I surfed around and found some more stuff about her. Several articles said she crochets and I saw the class in the course list for 'J term' and thought it might be something interesting to do. Then, I looked around online and found these really beautiful, luxury wooden crochet hooks, ordered one, and here I am." She'd waved it proudly, utterly sure that she was the center of everyone's attention. "Just glad my Furls Heirloom Wooden Hook arrived in time. Each hook is handmade, you see, costs about eighty dollars, and can take nearly a month to arrive. Well, the wooden ones, that is. Madison's fun lemon yellow one—hold it up for them to see, Maddy—they call them Candy Shop Hooks, how cute is that? Hers costs a little less and they cast them so they don't take as long to get. And then I noticed the little wooden yarn bowls and—oh dear!" Amy tittered. "I'm sounding like an infomercial! I should be saying, 'But that's not all!' But it is."

Ah, Amy. She just had to mention a famous person and how much her lovely and unique looking wooden crochet hook cost. I'd asked her about it after class and she'd said it was Bloodwood.

"Look," Amy said as she pulled a small shiny black box out of her designer tote bag. She opened the box and took out the hook. "When the light hits it one way, the grain of the wood gleams with this really lovely, rich golden-orangey glow. Can you see it?"

"Oh, yes!"

"But when you hold it at a different angle," she moved the hook slightly, "it's such a beautiful satiny deep red. Sometimes I'll just sit and look at it while I move it back and forth." She did just that as she spoke. "It's like a gem. If you don't have the angle right they look dark and dull, but when the light hits the facets, like it hits the grain in this wood, it gleams and sparkles."

It was one of those moments when a different side of Amy Twombly showed up. There had been less of the bubbly, brain-challenged blonde in her tone. She was serious and interesting in her appreciation of the hook's beauty.

While she was mesmerized by the play of light on the hook, I noticed a couple of cards had fallen out of the box and picked them up.

"Oh, thank you, Emory." Amy snatched them away from me, like she didn't want me to see them, but then showed them to me. "The black one is a business card. It's neat because you can see a selection of the Furls wooden hooks. The little yellow card is the info about my hook. They're all individually made and numbered."

She held the card over for me to see.

"See, it has the size listed, the kind of wood, and its number. Then on the left it has a greeting thingy and instructions on how to care for it. You use olive oil to keep the wood nice and smooth and stuff. I've already oiled it a couple of times, even though it says to do it once a month. I just … I enjoy how it feels in my hands."

I thanked her for showing the hook to me and explaining more about it. She put it back in its box, put the box in her tote, then left with Madison.

I'd never heard of such a wood and so I looked it up online. It's from South America but isn't an endangered tree, so that was good.

Now that I was remembering Amy's spiel that first day, it brought to mind that there had been something sort of nervous about the way Amy had been acting lately. She seemed more eager to please than usual. Not just wanting people to notice her but wanting to … what? Have them like her? She'd never seemed to care about people liking her before—only about impressing them.

I wondered …

Tsk, tsk, Emory girl. You've a class to teach. I pulled my mind back from Amy, her behavior, and her crochet hook, to the matter at hand.

"Everyone ready?"

"Yes, Mrs. Crawford," came a childish unison reply.

"Cute, you guys, real cute." I gave us all time to chuckle. "I taught myself this pattern by looking at an afghan Dr. Crawford and I got as a wedding gift from his Aunt Senia, so I always called it *Aunt Senia's Afghan Pattern.* I've since found out it has been around a while and is called *Crochet Diagonal Box.* For me, it's still Aunt Senia's Afghan Pattern. But, as I mentioned on Monday, you don't have to make an afghan. The pattern easily makes squares or rectangles, anything from square washcloths to king-sized afghans, scarves to table runners. So, I hope you've all decided what you want to make and we'll get started."

The class went on from there. We started at nine o'clock, took a half-hour break at eleven, then went from eleven-thirty to one-thirty. Since the class was an everyday technical class, we only met a half-day, allowing the afternoons for students to work on their projects. Academic "J term" classes, during the winter break, were either all day, five days a week, or all day Monday, Wednesday, and Friday.

Along with Amy was her daughter, Madison. I didn't know Madison as well as I knew the other Twombly kids. At fourteen she was considerably younger than my kids, but she seemed to be a nice young lady. She hadn't said much, either from shyness or because of being the youngest in the class, but neither had she been a problem like some youngsters can be when they are in a group that's all older people. I had Naomi Malkoff, whom I'd met last

June under what became distressing circumstances, but who had decided to stay here in Twombly. She was now an apprentice florist at Mysterious Ways: Plants, Herbs & Irish Blessings, working with my favorite local flower and plant expert, Aine McAllister. Tom Maxwell and Ed Ramsey were this year's token males. I always have at least one brave guy. The fellas played soccer on the Twombly College team and are fans of Steven Lenhart, a player for the San Jose Earthquakes—and an avid crocheter. They thought if it was cool enough for Steven it could be cool for them. I had three female college students, Tracy Watkins, Suzanne Cone, and Carrie Middlecoff, the girl who had been so perky about everyone having their patterns. And finally, Marge Purtle, my neighbor to the east at #1 Rigel Blvd. She'd been battling pneumonia and her doctor told her to let her assistants do the work at her accounting firm and take it easy for the month of January. She said it was either take a class for the month or go crazy. Since I was next door instead of somewhere else on campus, she felt my class would be a good, not strenuous, slow paced, doctor approved choice.

But Tracy and Suzanne weren't here. It seemed strange as they had been so enthusiastic.

It took the first hour of class to walk everyone through the pattern. It has a tricky spot in it that can be confusing to beginners, but I'd found over the years that I've taught the classes that Twombly students liked a challenge and quickly became bored if the pattern I chose was too simple. Finally, I was mostly walking around and saying, "Yes! You've got it," when, at about time for the break, we heard the upstairs door open and close followed by Tracy and Suzanne pelting down the stairs into the family room.

"Sorry we're late, Emory," Tracy puffed.

"Campus security is finally going to do something about it all,"

Suzanne gasped out in one breath.

"What?" said the class in Greek chorus unison.

"Here." I gestured to the empty sofa. "Sit down. Naomi, could you … Oh, you already have, thank you."

I gave each girl a glass of water as Naomi handed them to me.

"Slow down, now. Take a few deep breaths then tell us what the college is finally doing something about."

They sipped. They breathed. They calmed down to speak in longer sentences.

"The red things," Suzanne began. "The red things that have been appearing in our rooms at Mitchell dorm. It started happening in November, or thereabouts. It even took us a while before any of us said anything to each other."

"Red things appearing, not taken?" I asked.

"Yeah," Tracy nodded. "That's what made it so weird. I mean, breaking in to leave something is so much stranger than breaking in to *take* something. You know, taking is nearly normal."

"Totally." Suzanne shivered at the thought. "But at least now they're going to come to Mitchell and check out the rooms for scratch marks on the door jambs, finger prints and stuff."

"Well, I guess we'll be hearing more about this over our break. I've got lunch ready upstairs. Why don't the rest of you go on up and help yourselves while I get Tracy and Suzanne started on their afghans."

The group moved up the stairs, the two boys in the lead. I could hear Amy grumping as she went.

"I hope lunch is better today. Yesterday I'm positive the bread was stale and Monday the soup was over-cooked."

I started getting the two girls settled down and learning the pattern. But my brain was not fully on the stitching. The last time something around here got left where it shouldn't have been it was a strange dried flower arrangement on the welcome table for a conference and, soon after, there was a murder.

Chapter 2

JANUARY IN CENTRAL ILLINOIS! THERE MIGHT BE A BLIZZARD. IT might be warm enough that you're not sure whether to wear your winter coat or a heavy-ish spring jacket. Or it might be somewhere in between. Friday afternoon, three o'clock, Sophie and I were wandering about the Twombly College campus. It was a heavy-ish jacket day, an in-between day of too nice to not get some fresh air. The last snow had been three weeks ago and it was gone before Christmas. The ice-free sidewalks had beckoned to us both and walking a dog makes such a good motivator for getting one's rear end out of the house.

We walked past Blythe Hall on a sidewalk angling off to the northwest, toward the James E. Keeler Science Building where

Sophie's human daddy, my hubby Jebbin, has his office and beloved chemistry labs. Actually, the sidewalk ended in another of Twombly College's many and varied gardens. Between the science building and the Victor Herbert Music Building lies the J.M. Ramm Musical Garden and at the center of the garden the sidewalk diverges, taking pedestrians to the main entrance of either of the two buildings.

It really is a most unique place, dedicated to the idea that music is a mathematical science of sound and that science itself is the art of all the arts. There are statues and gizmos that use scientific principles to do ... well, whatever it was the art students and science students who worked together on them wished them to do. And there are whats-its and thingamy-bobs that produce sounds that have all been perfectly tuned so that all the "music" in the garden blends in ways pleasing to human hearing.

And in the garden sat Madison Twombly.

Cross-legged, working on her scarf for crochet class, she sat in a sunny spot on a bench beside the solar powered fountain that mixed the music of burbling water with the exotic tones of Tibetan Singing bowls as they randomly bumped each other while they floated around. She was wearing a stocking cap in the blue and gold of Twombly High School, where she's a freshman.

She was sniffling.

"Hi, Madison. The chill making your nose run?" I asked as Sophie and I walked over to her.

"Hmm? Oh, hi there, Mrs. Craw ... Emory." She dragged a coat sleeve across her nose in an effort to stop her sniffing. But that didn't do a thing for the tears on her cheeks. "No. Not the cold air."

She looked back down at her crocheting. She had chosen to make her scarf using a very soft acrylic yarn in Twombly College's green and gold.

"Your scarf is looking good." If she wanted to talk about the tears, well, I'd let her bring it up.

She held it up with a smile. "Yeah. Yeah, it is. Better than I thought it would. Shame the college soccer season is over, I'll just have to wear it next fall. Or," her smile widened, "I can wear it to the next equestrian event!" Her happy expression faded, though, as her arms sagged and the scarf made its way back to her lap. "Sometimes the arenas are cold. We go as often as we can 'cause Mama … Mama likes the horse shows. S-s-she s-says they … they're classy."

Okay, I'm a mother. So much for not butting in on her issues.

I sat down on the bench beside Madison as Sophie moved to her other side and nudged her head under the girl's right hand, offering convenient dog petting therapy. "I wasn't going to ask, but I could tell you've been crying." I handed her a hankie; I always carry one in my winter coat and jacket pockets for drips caused by cold air. "It's clean, no worries."

"Thanks."

"You don't ne …"

"I *want* to tell you what's wrong." She looked up with a jerk as she interrupted me, a look like panic in her eyes. Her right hand started to massage behind Sophie's floppy ears. "I've been wanting to tell someone for weeks now but just didn't know, you know, who I could … should …" Her hands flopped in frustration, her gaze shifted to the fountain. I managed to catch her scarf and bright yellow Furls hook before they slid from her lap to the sidewalk. "Sometimes it stinks being a Twombly! I mean, who can you say anything to without it getting all over town or over to the college people or back to Papa? Especially when it's …" She looked back at me, leaned in close, and whispered. "It's family stuff. Personal stuff."

"My father was a minister, Madison," I whispered in return. "I grew up knowing when and how to keep things to myself. That said, if I feel a need, would you mind if I share with Jebbin about it? I don't know anyone better at keeping a confidence than him and if I talk to him, then I'm not tempted to talk to anyone else. Will that be okay?"

Madison nodded with a weak little grin. "Yeah. I'm that way with my best friend, Diane. If we find out something, just sharing it with each other is all we need."

"Then what is it you need to get off your heart?"

"Resie Schmid."

"Your dad's new personal assistant?" I felt one of my shivers up the back. The name had just popped into my head, my internal voice saying it in unison with Madison. Oh, that? I have this gift. It used to trouble me, but Jairus, Madison's father, who has something way stronger, told me to embrace it. I try.

"Yes. Papa's always had a personal assistant, but this is the first time he's had a female one. She … She's really nice. Of course Cora and Jam VII haven't formed too much of an opinion about her since, well you know, Cora is married and Jam's away doing astronomy at University of Michigan. But they were both home at Thanksgiving and Christmas, well, Jam was home most of December on break, and I think they were feeling it too."

"Feeling what?"

"Everything is getting weird. I mean, at first she was just another personal assistant, but after a couple of weeks, Papa had her helping me with my homework, and then on her own she helped me with a couple of projects. She'd go and take care of baby John so Cora could have some alone time. She was packing and sending goodie boxes to Jam up in Ann Arbor. Stuff like that. Which at first we just thought was cool, but by Halloween, she was doing all the planning for the party we have every year at our house, plus the community Halloween party. And she'd sort of taken over the church ladies' group that Mama has over every month, and showing up at my school things, and ... I don't remember what all else. It's like she's trying to be our mother or something."

My tingling back was having a party of its own. Rabbit runnin' over my grave didn't touch this feeling. More like a herd of spiders were using my spine as a super highway. I could nearly see a huge, flashing neon sign "DANGER!" playing on my frontal cortex.

"Jairus, your dad, I mean—not your brother—he knows about all of this?"

Madison lowered her head. Her right hand left Sophie's head and the fingers of both hands started playing with her partially finished scarf, tugging it this way and that, straightening it out as it lay across her lap.

She nodded.

"He asked her to do it all. Or, well, he asked her to do most of it. Like I said, I think she has done some things on her own. Papa will ask her to do things while we're at the dinner table, with Mama and me sitting there hearing it all. She's the first PA who's taken her meals with us. Breakfast, lunch, and dinner, she's always there."

I'd had to lower my head to hear her above the ambient sounds of the Music Garden. Clearly, this was the heart of the matter. I had to ask what I had to ask.

"Do you think your dad and the PA, Resie, are ..."

"No." The still quiet voice. A delicate little sigh. "I really don't, 'cause I thought about it really early on and started, you know, watching for anything, like ..." Her pause was long, her voice tight when she spoke again. "Like touching or sexy glances from either one of them. Anything that were double entendre type phrases, but, no." She sat up straighter, set her shoulders, and took a deep breath in through her nose. Her hand went back to petting Sophie. "No. I'm sure Papa's not doing that. But, I think Mama thinks Resie is trying to get him to." She threw me a challenging look. "You know Mama. Most everyone says she's a bitch."

Ah, hence the challenge in her eyes. Would I disagree with her? I needed to be diplomatic on this.

"I know she seems snobby and bossy. I know she comes across like she doesn't have much concern for other people unless it makes her look good to someone she wants to impress. And I know she usually manages to be on better behavior when your dad is around."

I paused. The challenge was still there waiting for me to address it. My turn to take a breath, adjust my posture, and settle myself.

"Having said that, I'll say that no, I don't think she's a bitch. I think she plays the part well. I think she plays a lot of parts well. I try to never forget she was a theater arts major."

The youngster on the bench beside me relaxed.

"She's scared. I really think she's scared." Madison looked away again, her challenge to me over. "I hear her talking out loud to herself, which she didn't do before. I caught her going through some of Papa's financial books in early October. I noticed that's what they were because she was saying something about, 'She thinks I'm a ditz, but I know what she's up to. I bet there's money missing. She's gonna find out who she's up against if I find there's money missing.' It was all anger then, I think, but now she's angry and scared. With Resie being so nice to me, Cora, and Jam VII, I've heard bits of things like, 'My kids love me. I'm sure they do,' said in a way where you know she's trying to convince herself."

Madison picked up and looked at her crocheting, took the lemon yellow hook in her hand, and rubbed her fingers along its smooth, glossy surface.

"I think that's what all this is about, Mrs. Craw … Emory. That's why the crocheting and offering to buy me a really cool hook and the yarn bowl and everything if I'd take the class with her. You know, like I wouldn't figure out that it's because Resie has been doing stuff with me and Mama hasn't done much since I was a little kid. She's been acting sicky-sweet-gooey nice at home when Papa or Resie are around but like she's having some sort of mega-bitch meltdown when they aren't. Well, until lately. Since Christmas she's been trying to be gooey-sweet nice all the time. Not that she manages it." The tiniest hint of a smile didn't quite reach her worried eyes, but it did quirk the corner of her mouth. "I think it's hard to change and she is so totally overdoing it. Like on Wednesday she insulted your lunches when we all went upstairs but you had stayed down to show Tracy and Suzanne …"

She looked over toward the entrance from the campus into the garden like a hunting dog on point.

"Papa's coming."

I was thinking about her having her father's gift of insight, of knowing things he should have no way of knowing, when the man himself strode into the garden.

"Good, Sweetie, you're here like I thought. You need to come home with me right now." Jairus finally glanced at me. "Hello, Emory."

"Papa …"

"A girl from Mitchell Dorm is missing. Until she's found I don't want you wandering around alone. Please, gather your stuff up and let's go."

Jairus turned to me.

"We'll talk later, Emory. You might better check in with Jebbin. I don't know when he'll expect to be needed. There will be evidence from the girl's room to analyze. All I know is she's one of the girls who's had red items left in her room. There'll be those to have a look at if nothing else." He hesitated. "You both know her, I think."

"The crochet class." I just knew.

"Tracy Watkins." All three of us said the girl's name, leaving us looking at each other as an otherworldly tension hung in the air with the late afternoon chill. When she and Suzanne had told the class about the mysterious red "gifts", she hadn't mentioned that she'd been a recipient.

Jairus turned back to his daughter. "Got your stuff, Honey?"

She nodded, and he gently took her arm and started off down the sidewalk.

"Bye, Emory! Thanks for everything! Dr. Crawford, Papa, and you will help find Tracy," she called back over her shoulder just before they turned to the right and out of sight, heading toward the parking lot on the far side of the music building.

Chapter 3

I WENT INTO THE SCIENCE BUILDING AND HEADED TO THE CHEM-istry department on the third floor. Biology had the first floor with easy access to the outside for the environmental sciences classes and the botany classes. Physics was on the second floor along with the mathematics, computer sciences, earth sciences, and astron-omy departments. Chemistry had the top because they usually had the smelliest, most toxic experiments and this way the filtered air vents channeled their results a short direct route out of the labs via the roof.

I took the stairs, even though I was wanting to hurry and couldn't run up all six flights. I have to get *some* exercise and it was good for Sophie too.

Yes. Sophie goes to see Jebbin in his office.

At the top of the stairs, Jebbin's office is to the left and at the end of the hall, with the door set into an angled corner. All the corner offices had their entrances in these offset walls. I knocked, Sophie woofed, and we waited for a "come in" before opening the door. Jebbin was sitting at his desk, which formed a triangle with the corner opposite the door. There were no windows set into those corners, so nobody had to talk to a figure silhouetted against the glare of un-curtained windows. He had built a triangular table, which fit into the corner to use as a credenza, the top of which was even with one of the shelves of the two built-in bookshelves that formed the corner. It held his printer, coffee maker and supplies, iPod speaker, his graduated beaker coffee mug, and a photo of our family.

His desk wasn't nearly as tidy. It was strewn with books, chemistry journals, a photo of Lanthan and Felysse with our grandchildren, a new photo of Molly with Freddy, and a photo of me and him with our instruments at a bluegrass festival.

"Woof," he said to Sophie, who pricked up her ears and tipped her head to one side. "And hello, Hon."

I lifted my eyebrows. "You're sitting there calmly so I'm assuming you haven't heard."

"About the kidnapping? Yeah, I heard about ten minutes ago from Jairus. How do you know?"

"I was in Ramm Garden talking to Madison Twombly when her father came to take her home."

"Hmm …" Jebbin sat back in his chair and tented his fingers. "I can see that. I'd have done the same if Molly was still around here."

I sat in the wing-backed chair on the visitor's side of the desk. Sophie went around the desk to sit by her daddy.

"And you're just sitting here, why? Since, you know, I expected you to be doing … I'm not sure what, but not just sitting here."

He grinned. "Am I a Crime Scene Tech? No, I'm not. They bring the stuff to me and I do my thing with it in the lab. I got off the phone just before you knocked and it should …"

A solid thump shook the oak office door.

"… be here any minute." He finished his sentence. "Come on in."

I'm sorry to say it was Captain Henry Schneider who strode into the room carrying a medium-sized cardboard box. The head of homicide at the Golden County Sheriff's Department wasn't a big fan of Jebbin. Nor of me for that matter.

"Here's the …" The Captain noticed me and scowled. "Oh, Lord. You're in here. We don't need you messin' about with this. This is an active situation. No dead body that isn't going anywhere, we need to find a girl before she's turned into a dead body. No room for armchair meddlers slowing us down."

He had such finesse with words.

"Good afternoon to you, too, Captain Schneider." I could have been snottier, but I hoped I might get to stay if I behaved myself.

"Ahem!" Jebbin got our attention. "My office, Captain. My wife. My dog. My decision." He leaned both forearms on the edge of his desk and gave Henry a gentle smile, but his eyes were sparking with humor behind his glasses. "What do you have for me to look at?"

I really did try not to look too smug as I sat back in the chair.

Henry closed his eyes and stood there like he was posing for a sculptor. His eyes remained closed when he spoke.

"I have red things her roommate says weren't …" He opened his eyes and looked at me in a way that pleaded with me to leave.

"Tracy's." I filled in for him. "She … is in my crocheting class and I already know she's the missing girl."

"Yeah. Well." Henry looked into the box. "They aren't Tracy's. Weird things. An un-inflated red balloon. Round shaped, not like a condom or something like that. A red golf ball. I mean, where on earth do you get red golf balls? And six more things. The room-mate said Tracy'd gotten more of this junk than anyone else, so far. Here." He plopped the box on Jebbin's desk with a thud and stuck a clipboard in front of his face. "It's all yours as soon as you sign for it. Items are all listed on the form. We didn't do a bunch of separate sheets, but they're all bagged and numbered individually."

Jebbin signed the sheet and handed back the clipboard.

"I suppose you're gonna let her look through it all?" He held his right hand up like a cop directing traffic to stop. "No. Nope. Don't tell me. I really don't want to know. Like you said. Your office. Your little scientific, antiseptic, sterile world where, yep, they're all your decisions." He then walked out, though I caught his mutter: "Whole crime fighting world is goin' to hell in a handcart." He gave me one last look before he closed the door.

"Can I see?" I sounded as much like an eager kindergartener as I could.

"Yes, little Emory. You can look if you're a good girl and don't open any of the baggies yourself, and don't touch the things inside them."

"Yippee!"

We both got up, Sophie too, to take the box to the lab.

Jebbin paused to look around, as though he was forgetting something.

"What?" I asked.

"Where's the handcart that you're taking the whole of investigative procedure to hell in?"

I linked my arm through his. "I left it at home."

It was dark as we walked home across the campus. All the items had been clean except for Tracy's fingerprints on the items that would hold prints. Just a flat, round red balloon, a red #1 Icicles brand golf ball, a red velvet ribbon, a two-inch-tall stuffed red dog, a red *maneki-neko* figurine—I had rarely seen one of those Japanese beckoning cat figures in red—a Bicycle brand Queen of Hearts playing card, a one-inch-diameter shiny red button, and a red colored bottle of bubble liquid with a red blowing wand. Technically that made nine red things, but the police had counted the blowing wand and the bottle of bubble liquid as all one item.

We finally got home, ordered a pizza, and then sat at the kitchen table in silence while we waited for it to arrive.

No one had seen or heard from Tracy.

Chapter 4

JEBBIN AND I FINALLY WENT TO BED AROUND MIDNIGHT, HAVING stayed up long enough for our dinner to settle while hoping for a call about Tracy. Even then we cuddled together and continued to talk until I drifted off to sleep.

I was dreaming about some sort of primitive, native person sending out drum signals when Hortense jumped on me, Kumquat yowled, and Sophie started tugging at the blankets. I emerged from sleep enough to realize the drumbeats were real.

The drumbeats were someone knocking at the door. My clock said it was five in the morning.

I grabbed my robe as I dashed toward the living room and looked through the peephole in the front door. I hated using the thing, with its funky fisheye view, but we'd put it in especially for me, years ago. The windows in the old oak front door are too high for me to look through. I mostly saw a red cowboy hat. Leaving the chain hooked up, I opened the door.

"Hello?" I tried to sound more awake than I felt.

"Am I late for crocheting?" the red hat said before the head it sat upon was tilted back enough for the wearer and me to look at each others' faces.

It was Tracy. She swayed.

"Oh my ...!" I cut myself off as she reeled back as though I'd shoved her. I had shouted with my surprise at seeing her and she looked befuddled and frightened. I closed the door enough to loose the chain, then opened it wide. "Tracy, Hon." I said her name gently. "You aren't late at all, Sweetie. Just come on in and we'll have something to eat until it's time for class." I didn't tell her there wasn't any class today since it was Saturday. I thought it would have just confused her more.

She didn't move, just stood there swaying in a tiny circular way, so I stepped out, took her by the arm, and drew her into the house, quietly shutting the door behind us. My brain clicked—red cowboy hat. Red. I checked out the rest of her outfit. She wore a red Western-style shirt, blue jeans, and red cowboy boots. Lots of red. She wobbled like a buzzed drunk, not staggering but unbalanced. I led her to the kitchen table, so much more welcoming and cozy, I felt, than the dining table, and sat her so she could look out the window over the sink. I needed to get Jebbin but wanted to get Tracy settled first.

"Do you like coffee, Tracy?"

"Hmm? Oh ... ah ... Yes. Yes I do ... Cream ... I like it with cream, please."

I was growing more concerned by the moment. Her speech sounded as drunk as her walking looked.

"I take mine with cream and sweetener," I jabbered away at her. "I'll just get the coffee maker going here and then I need to use the bathroom." I had a sudden thought. "Do you need to go while I'm getting the coffee going?"

"Yes," she said, and nothing more as she stared out the window.

"I think you all usually use the one downstairs when you're here for class. I'll show you where the one up here is."

She stood up and followed me down the short hall that led past the laundry room, the main bathroom, and to the hall to the right, where the doors to all the bedrooms are. As Tracy went into the bathroom and shut the door I noticed she was touching the walls to steady herself. I went into the master bedroom to wake up Jebbin.

"Tracy's here?" he asked as soon as he was awake enough to understand what I was saying to him.

"Yes. She was knocking on the door this morning at five o'clock. The cats and Sophie woke me up. She's in the bathroom right now, but I've got the coffee maker going and I'll sit her back at the kitchen table when she comes out. Just you get up and out there asap."

His eyes were alert and fully awake as he saluted me. "Yes, ma'am. I'll call Jairus and the police station from in here before I come out." He paused a moment. "I'm surprised Jairus hasn't already called or shown up. His radar must be broken."

"Maybe," I said. As I headed out of the room and back to the kitchen I wondered about a possible glitch in the Twombly gift of knowing when something important happened before anyone had time to call Jairus. I'd only been in the kitchen a few minutes when I heard the shower in the main bathroom running.

Tracy must have gotten into the shower.

A shower! Ruined evidence!

I ran to the door and opened it. She was standing next to the tub in her underwear, the red cowboy clothes scattered on the floor around her feet. How was I going to handle this? Would she fall apart if I asked what had happened to her? I had to say something; we couldn't lose the trace evidence that might be on her.

"Ah, Tracy. Honey, you shouldn't take a shower just now."

She looked at me then at the clothes on the floor. "I don't want these, Mrs. Crawford. I ... they aren't mine." Tracy looked back up at me and I finally noticed that her pupils were dilated. She had probably been drugged. No wonder she was having trouble talking and responding.

"Of course they aren't," I said as I maneuvered around her to shut off the water. "I noticed they're a bit big for you, aren't they?"

She nodded. "Yes. They ... don't fit. I don't like them."

She paused a long time but I didn't say anything.

"They were ... just there ... and I had to change."

Tracy twitched.

She gasped.

Her shoulders jerked as her eyes opened wide. Large tears started running from her eyes.

"Mrs. ... Emory. They aren't ... They aren't my clothes. They're ... They're ..." She looked at the pile on the floor. "I had to ... had to change. I don't know ... where they came from." Her knees gave way and I managed to catch her enough to ease her descent to the fuzzy rug in front of the tub.

"It's going to be okay, Tracy. You just shouldn't take a shower yet, Sweetie."

"Can't ..." She sobbed. "Can't put them ..."

"No, no, Hon. No. You don't have to put them back on." I straightened up, moved the small distance to the linen closet, and took out a full-length pink chenille robe that was on one of the shelves. "Here you go. You just put this on, Hon. It's all fresh and clean. My mom used to keep a robe on hand for company and I just followed suit when I had my own home." I wrapped the robe around her shoulders. "Do you need help putting it on?"

She shook her head, but couldn't find the sleeves as she reached around, so I held it out and helped her slip both arms into place, sat her up a little straighter, crossed the front closed over her, and tied the belt.

"There ya go," I said. "My mom always said you never knew when a guest might show up soaked from a sudden downpour or need to spend the night unexpectedly, so she always kept two spare robes in the bathroom closet; one for a man and one for a woman. Over the years I've been amazed how often they've come in handy."

I helped Tracy to her feet. She hung onto me and cried some more. I held her for a while before easing back to give her a smile and dab some of the tears off her cheeks.

"You ready for some coffee?"

"Yeah." She managed a hint of a grin, but a haunted look still shadowed her eyes.

Jebbin was at the coffee maker as we walked into the kitchen and it gave Tracy a start to see someone else in the room. He just took it in stride, smiled, and pointed to the table.

"There's a mug of coffee for you, Tracy, and all the fixin's so you can have it how you like it. I put a couple of ice cubes in it so you can drink it right away. It won't burn ya." He moved a tad slower than usual to sit down where he'd pulled one of the chairs to the end of the table so he wouldn't be right next to her. "I don't think we've met. I usually go to my office when Emory has her 'J term' craft classes, and I don't think I've had you for a chem class. I'm Dr. Crawford."

Tracy's hand shook as she poured cream into her coffee. She used both hands to hold it steady and drank it all before setting the mug down to peer at my husband as though she couldn't keep him in focus.

"No." She paused. She was obviously still dazed. "No, I haven't taken chem. I … I haven't met you but … I've seen you."

She swayed sharply and nearly fell off her chair as the doorbell rang. She was too out of it to jump when it startled her. Jebbin had made those phone calls and in a couple of moments he escorted Jairus and Captain Henry into the kitchen along with two women I didn't recognize, one in maybe her fifties, the other gray-haired.

"Tracy!" the younger woman squealed.

"Mom! Gran!" Tracy rose and stumbled into a group hug.

Much as I didn't like the man, I motioned to Henry to follow me down the hall to the bathroom.

"I got to her just in time to keep her from taking a shower," I said quietly, gesturing at the clothes-strewn floor. "I'm sorry she took the clothes off and they've been on our floor, but I figure the crime scene techs can take the throw rug with them and vacuum up a sample of what all is on the floor. It should have been pretty clean. We don't use it much, we use the master bath, and my crochet class students usually use the bathroom downstairs."

To my great surprise, Henry didn't say anything snide. He just nodded his head, pulled out his cell, and called the station to send out the techs while I went back to the kitchen. I guess he couldn't find fault with my handling of the situation … or was just grateful I'd kept her from showering in case the worst had happened?

The doorbell rang again and I went to let in the paramedics and showed them the way to the kitchen. They showed impressive skill with the way they got Tracy's mom and grandmother to let go of her so they could check the girl out. Questions were asked and answered, a clip on her finger measured her heart rate and oxygen levels while her pupil responses were checked with a penlight. The crime scene techs arrived next and disappeared into the bathroom to start bagging and tagging the clothes and our throw rug.

Then they were all gone: Jairus, Captain Henry, Tracy in the pink chenille robe, her family, paramedics, and techs. And Jebbin too, with a peck on my cheek and an "Off to start my forensics."

I looked around at our pets, who had arrived to be let out, in Sophie's case, and get fed, in Hortense's and Kumquat's case. "I will be interviewing you all later," I said to them as I opened the door onto the screened porch and then the door to the small deck with the stairs down to the yard. "I will expect you all to tell me everything you know."

Sophie was down the stairs before I finished my sentence. She'd been a very patient and controlled girl but had reached her limit.

As I got the kitties their morning treat, I started thinking of how I was going to find out what Tracy told the authorities when they questioned her.

Chapter 5

BY THE TIME ALL THE EXCITEMENT WAS OVER IT WAS NEARLY 7:00 a.m. I fixed myself some breakfast, got dressed, made myself presentable, bundled up, and headed to the library by 8:55 a.m. I'm off my regular library volunteer schedule during "J term" because of teaching the crochet class, but there is always something that needs to be put away or tidied in a library so no one complains if a volunteer just shows up. Seeing as it was Saturday, the public library sections were pretty busy. There is something for children every Saturday from ten in the morning until four in the afternoon all year round. Twombly isn't the biggest town, but it's big enough to have four elementary schools that feed into its junior high school and high school. Of course, junior high and high school add in the kids bussed in from the smaller towns nearby.

The college parts of the library were quieter. Although many of our students return to campus early after Christmas break, they don't all take "J term" classes, and my craft classes aren't the only ones that don't demand a lot of "book learnin'."

I stuck my head into the head librarian's office, not really expecting to see my best friend, AnnaMay Langstock, sitting at her desk—but she was.

"Greetings, oh great and powerful head of the library." I bowed as I entered.

"Greetings?" her tone was appropriately superior. "Mere greetings? 'Reverence, oh great and powerful …' 'Adoration, oh great and powerful …' Get with it, plebeian minion."

We laughed as I plopped into her visitor's chair.

"So, why did the kidnapped girl show up at your house this morning?"

Had it been anyone else, I would have been shocked.

Had it been anyone else, I would have wondered if they had intuition like Jairus Twombly's or even a lesser version like mine.

But this was AnnaMay. Former Air National Guard staff sergeant. She likes nice, tidy, tangible explanations.

"Suzanne Cone." AnnaMay, enjoying my confused look, filled me in. "She's Tracy's best friend. She knows Tracy's mom, who came into Twombly last night late after getting the call about her daughter having gone missing. Suzanne knows Cindy, our front desk student volunteer who seems to be here too much of the time to actually be taking classes. I heard all about it from Cindy."

"O … K," I said, suitably impressed with my friend's network. "Tracy showed up at our house because she didn't know what day it was and thought it was time for the crocheting class. Which doesn't start at five in the morning while it's still dark outside, but she was a little too drugged out for that to register."

"Drugged?"

"Slow movements, dilated pupils, distracted replies to questions. So, yeah. I figured she'd been given something."

AnnaMay nodded. "Logical conclusion. Why'd you stick your head in my office? I'm not usually here on Saturday, or well, at least not this early."

"I was going to tell you my news that you already knew." I let her gloat a moment. "Any ideas on how I can find out what the police get out of Tracy when they question her?"

"Which police? City or county?"

"Captain Henry Schneider of the Golden County Sheriff's Department."

AnnaMay came as close to rolling her eyes as she would ever get. "You haven't got a prayer, Emory. I'm not even sure God could move that man to share anything with you or Jebbin that he doesn't have to. Shame it wasn't the city cops, although Jason might not have handled the case anyway."

Jason was Detective Jason Anderson of the Twombly City Police, who, unlike Captain Henry, was a good friend of Jebbin and me.

"No, he probably would have gotten it. Like Henry is for the county, he's the best detective on the city force. He'd get a big case like a kidnapping. All I would need to do is invite him over for a lasagna dinner and he might tell me everything they have, the dear man."

"Ah, well," AnnaMay sighed in mock sympathy, "I guess you'll just have to find a recipe that works as well on Henry. Are you here to work, or just here to tell me old news?"

"Work. I need to do something other than sit home and stew over this. Lucky Jebbin has evidence to work on."

"Then, my library slave, go ye forth and shelve books! An entire cartful awaits you out by the front desk."

I stood and backed my way out of her office, bowing repeatedly as I went. "I hear and obey, oh great and powerful one!"

"You obey?" she quipped as I was closing the door. "That'll be the day!"

I was on my second cartload of books over in the public library area, sitting on one of those step stools that roll until you put weight on them, taking a break to read *The 500 Hats of Bartholomew Cubbins* by Dr. Seuss, when I heard my name being hissed.

"Pssst! Mrs. Crawford. Emory."

I glanced around wondering who was being so covert. Really. It's no secret that I work in the library so there was no need in that regard to whisper my name, and I don't know of too many libraries that are as heavy handed with the no talking rule as they were when I was a kid.

"Over here," the whispering voice continued. "On the other side of the stack to your right."

I looked through the gap between the tops of books and the underside of the shelves to my right and saw Madison. She had to be on her knees as her face was even with mine.

"Hi, Madison. You don't need to whisper," I said in a quiet but normal voice. "Why don't you just come over here?"

She chuckled. "I'm having fun playing at being undercover. Part of it is I'm not supposed to be here and I have to hurry back to the hospital. I do volunteer work on Saturdays and I'm only on my break. Just wanted to let you know to meet me for lunch." She glanced at her watch. "It's eleven now. I'll be done for the day at one. Can you meet me at Quaint Cuisine? I have a recording of Tracy's interview with Captain Henry."

"You have what!" I wasn't sure I should believe her or not.

Madison winked in reply. "You heard me. Will you be there?"

"With bells on." I paused a moment. "No, that'd attract too much attention. I'll be there with my secret decoder ring."

The poor child looked blank.

"You're too young to remember those. I'll be there. Now, get out of here before you get caught away from the hospital."

We grinned at each other and she hurried off.

I got caught up helping at the checkout desk and so was late arriving at Quaint Cuisine, which is exactly what the name says. The building is mid- to late-1800s like most of downtown Twombly. It has one dining area, tastefully simple, with decor of high-end antiques in a space defined by marble floors and dark oak wainscoting that has the perfect feel for business lunches. Another section is intermixed with an eclectic shop. The section with the shop has all sorts of fanciful murals and figures painted on the walls, making the shop and its part of the eatery feel more artsy and casual.

The food is the same—upscale, health-conscious cuisine—in both dining areas. Freshly made sandwiches on handmade hearty white, multigrain, or rye rolls, or croissants include extras like baby romaine lettuce leaves, freshly sliced tomato, sliced mushrooms, sliced hard boiled eggs, deli dill pickle spears, sliced purple onion, and Swiss, Co-Jack, and Pepper-Jack cheeses. And there are salads. Freshly made green salads are available with all the same goodies that go on the sandwiches. They'll add any of the sandwich meats—freshly sliced ham, turkey, or beef—to your salad as well as the chicken salad or tuna salad that gets used for sandwiches. Then, there are several different pasta salads with different shapes of pasta, diced raw veggies, and succulent dressings on them, as well as a seven-layer salad that's to die for.

They don't offer as many dessert choices, but have excellent chocolate chip and oatmeal raisin cookies, carrot cake bars, and a pie of the day.

I started to look for Madison when my cell phone signaled a text message.

Look on the mezzanine.

I looked up to see Madison looking down. Then she tapped at her phone.

I've got a table up here in the far corner of the shop section, her text read. *Get your lunch and come on up.*

There was a pause, then, *I didn't want to yell down to you. ;-)* came through.

I smiled, gave her the "okay" signal, and went to the drink and ordering line. After placing my order I went up the elegant staircase in the "business lunch" part of the restaurant. That part of the "Quaint Cuisine" had been a bank in its former life and this grand wood and marble staircase, rising along the wall separating the bank from the shop, once led to the bank offices on the mezzanine level. The former bank president's office, now labeled "The President's Room," was the only enclosed area left, and the restaurant used it for people who wanted privacy for group luncheons. The walls for the other offices had been removed so the upper level had a nice, breezy, open feel. The balustrades were all the same dark oak as the wainscoting on the main floor and the staircase, with a brass topper to match the stair's brass handrail. At the end of the business area's upper level, furthest from the shop part of the restaurant and near "The President's Room," an elevator had been added to allow for handicapped access to that level and the meeting room. Beside the elevator was a counter. A walkway led back from there to where a dumbwaiter carried the trays upstairs from the serving area. I waited until the staff person there brought my tray, then went to find Madison.

As on the main floor, an arched doorway had been cut through the bank's thick wall to connect into the restaurant/shop section, which had always been a shop with hardwood floors and pressed tin ceilings. The mezzanine in there had a wrought iron railing and supports, with a wide wrought iron circular staircase at the far end.

Madison was at a table by a tall window at the front of the building, in the far corner .

"You are going to be so thrilled," she exclaimed sotto voce.

"Do I want to know how you managed to do this?" I was taking my green salad with tuna salad and all sorts of other veggie goodies and my raspberry spritzer off my tray. "I mean, I'm glad you got the information, but you didn't do anything illegal …" I finally looked her in the eye, "… did you?"

She thought a moment before answering even more softly than she had spoken before. "Well. I suppose it might be." She fiddled with her fork then looked up at me with her eyes twinkling. "Next time I'll just listen and take it all down in shorthand. I don't think that gets treated the same as a mechanical or digital recording."

I stopped with a forkful of salad part way to my mouth, wondering if I'd heard her correctly. "You know shorthand?"

"Yeah. I read about it in a novel and thought it sounded interesting. So, I looked online and found out you can take online courses in it, and I took one. Gregg Shorthand. It's lots of fun, really, and I can take notes at school way faster."

"You, my dear, are an odd fourteen-year-old," I said just before taking my first bite of lunch.

She smiled and nodded. "Yep! And proud of it. There's several of us at school, you know, 'nerds,' who get a kick out of learning and doing things kids our age don't usually do. Like using a tablet computer and a smart phone to listen in on conversations."

"Okay. Spill it. You did what?" I put my forkful of salad into my mouth without being able to appropriately savor it as my attention was totally on Madison.

"I found an article online once about what to do if you're staying somewhere with your baby and need a baby monitor but don't have one. You set up two Skype accounts. Log into one of them on your iPad or whatever tablet you use, log into the other one on your iPhone or smartphone of your choice, use the tablet one to call the phone one and—hey! Presto! You have a baby monitor. You just leave the iPad by the crib. Use the mute function on your phone so noise on your end doesn't get picked up and you're all set. You need an app to do the recording; most phones don't come with a recording feature. I've used it a few times to listen in on my parents."

Madison paused and quickly looked away to her right at the long line of tables along the windows, then down at her sandwich, obviously uncomfortable, before continuing.

"Maybe I shouldn't have admitted that. It was when I thought maybe Dad and Resie … I felt bad though and only did it those couple of times." She sighed then looked at me and grinned. "So I knew it would work. I just left my iPad facedown on the nightstand beside the bed; the microphone still picks everything up. I stuck my phone in the pocket of my smock and nobody was the wiser. Despite what I said a bit ago, I'm not too worried about legal issues. I've done my research on that, too. Technically, my recording device was in plain view so I wasn't secretly listening, even though Captain Schneider and cohorts didn't know it was on. He probably didn't even notice it or if he did he might have thought it was the doctor's. Some of them carry tablets for taking notes. That and I asked Tracy if I could record the conversation before they came in from talking to the doctors and her mom."

I nearly ended up with raspberry spritzer up my nose as I choked slightly. "You ... You ..." I coughed to clear my throat. "You asked Tracy? In her condition you expect that to hold water?"

Madison grinned again. "Of course. I also carry a little voice recorder in my smock for when I'm going to get a long string of orders from a nurse or doctor. I turned it on and asked her, 'Tracy, is it okay if Madison Twombly listens in on your talk with Captain Schneider?' She said ..."

Madison pulled the small unit out of her purse and punched in some instructions.

"Tracy, is it okay if Madison Twombly listens in on your talk with Captain Schneider?"

I could barely hear the words; she must have had the volume way down.

"That's ... That's strange. You're Madison Twombly ... Aren't you?"

"Yes. Will it be okay with you?"

"Yeah. After all, you're nearly a nurse ... or something. You have scrubs on. Sure."

Madison turned the unit off.

"There. Permission from someone who is over seventeen and therefore an adult." She looked at her watch. "I gotta head home. I'm worried about my Mom especially since it's just her and Resie at home. I'll email the recording to you. I haven't listened to it yet. Hopefully tonight. Oh! What's your email?"

She turned on her phone, I gave her my email, and she typed it into her *Notes* app, and with a wave and a "Bye!" she was gone.

I didn't enjoy my lunch.

I didn't taste my lunch.

My mind was too busy with thoughts of a dubiously obtained recording, permission from a young person whom I knew was still under the influence of drugs, of possible reactions from the ever friendly Captain Henry ... and Madison being so worried because her mother was home alone with "the other woman" in her family's life.

Chapter 6

I WENT HOME.

I had originally planned on going back to the library but now I had a recording to listen to.

Should I listen to it?

Would that make me guilty of complicity?

Would my concerns ever stop going round and round in my head?

I let myself in my front door.

"Hi, Hon!"

My gasped shriek echoed off the walls.

Really, it was only Jebbin, but a Jebbin I wasn't expecting to be there and since my mind had been on drugged coeds and sneaky teenagers with Captain Henry thrown into the mix, my mind automatically assumed I was in trouble. Silly mind. Well, it was either all that or just being startled.

His expression all concern, Jebbin hurried over to me. "I'm sorry, Honey. I didn't mean to make you scream." He pointed under the dining table where our Golden Retriever was cowering. "You frightened Sophie like I frightened you. Sorry. You gonna be okay?"

I nodded, breathed, and squatted down to be closer to eye level with Sophie. "It's okay, girl. Mama didn't mean to scare the good doggie by deafening her. Come here, Soph. Come here, it's okay."

With due caution Sophie crawled out from under the table, walked as softly as she could toward Jebbin and me, sniffed us both, then sat down with a sigh as I stood up.

"I was expecting an empty house, that's all. Are you home for lunch?"

"Yeah." He turned and headed toward the kitchen. "Yeah. I was throwing a sandwich together when I heard the door open."

I looked at the pieces of sandwich on the floor just as Sophie noticed them. She proceeded to eat the evidence of the effect of my shriek.

"Throwing being the operative word, I see." We both chuckled. "Sit down and I'll fix you another. I had lunch at Quaint Cuisine."

"I'll get myself something to drink. Were you by yourself?" he asked as he walked to the refrigerator then dug around inside it.

I thought fast. "No. AnnaMay was with me." I didn't think he needed to know about my meeting with Madison. After all, what if she got into trouble over all of this?

Jebbin raised an eyebrow at me as he reappeared from the depths of the fridge with a diet Vernors ginger ale.

"You aren't, ah, *looking into* the incident with Tracy, are you? I mean beyond being my lab assistant last night?"

"No. I wanted something to distract me, actually, from all the excitement of her showing up on our doorstep this morning. After everyone left I had breakfast and went to the library to ..." I waved my hands about in a vacant sort of way. "To do whatever. There's always stuff to do and I needed stuff to do. I talked to AnnaMay and we decided to do lunch."

"Hmm," my husband grunted as he sat down at his place at the table where I'd just placed his replacement sandwich. He popped open his Vernors too close to his face and started coughing. It has to be the most carbonated beverage in existence and usually he knew better than to inhale too close to the can right after opening it. Neither of us grew up with Vernors. It wasn't available in Missouri, where Jebbin's from, and I didn't have it until I was in high school and my father pastored a church in Ypsilanti, Michigan. I fell in love with it and I was thrilled when I found it for sale at the IGA grocery store in Twombly a few years ago. Now we both prefer it to any other ginger ale—despite its enthusiastic carbonation.

"Whew!" he said when he'd caught his breath. "Good stuff! Once it stops attacking you."

We shared the laugh we always share over things that have become family "inside" jokes. It's a certain warm, comfortable sound that is part humor and a lot love.

"So," I said as I sat at my place across the table from my hubby. "What's happenin' at the lab today?"

"I've been going over trace on Tracy's ... 'trace on Tracy's,' sounds weird but you know what I mean ..." He took some time out to eat before continuing. "I've been going over the clothes with two advanced forensics students. We think they were washed before she wore them. There's some stuff on them, there's always stuff on clothes, but not as much as we were expecting for the worn condition of the items. We think they came from used clothing shops because of the amount of wear. The only item with much trace evidence on it was the cowboy hat and even that might not be of much help. Horsehair, bits of straw, bits of hay, lots of sweat that we'll analyze but, depending on the hat's history, we reckon it won't be much help. Even if it was only worn by one other person we've no reason to assume that person's DNA is on record. And if the most recent trip to the secondhand store wasn't its first …. well, we'll get a hodgepodge of samples."

I nodded. "Hopefully Tracy will remember something helpful."

Jebbin looked at me. I could see the discussion going on in his head as he chewed another bite of sandwich. He was trying to decide whether or not he should say much to me about the parts of the case he wasn't directly involved in. And I think I saw a few concerns about telling me his own lab information flit by in his mind as well. Then, his expression settled.

"Our update, late this morning, was that she hadn't made a whole lot of sense yet and they were gonna let her rest for the day and try again this evening."

"That makes sense. Let whatever he gave her work out of her system. Speaking of that, do they know what it was yet?"

"Antonia is doing the pathology work, as per usual, and she always gives priority status to major cases, and kidnapping counts as major. She found traces of flunitrazepam. With Tracy still acting drunk this long after she was taken, Antonia suspected a date-rape type drug might have been used so she looked for them first." He reached across the table and covered my hand with his. "I should have said this sooner. A date-rape drug maybe, but she wasn't raped. So, at least she won't have to deal with that. Back to the flunitrazepam. It's a fairly quick acting, long lasting sedative-type drug, which was why she was still acting so out of it even though it might have been administered some time yesterday afternoon."

Jebbin paused but this time it wasn't to eat. His hand stayed on mine and after a few seconds he looked up at me.

"A major side effect of flunitrazepam that the other date-rape drugs don't have is that it causes amnesia, primarily affecting the time just before, during, and after its highest levels of potency. Which usually works out to be the time the perpetrator first comes into contact with the victim, the time of the crime, and the time afterward until the drug starts losing its strength in the system. There's a good chance that she won't remember very much about the whole incident."

We talked a little more, he gave me a kiss goodbye, and I was left to listen to a tape that might not reveal nearly as much information as Madison and I had hoped.

Fifteen minutes later I was done listening.

It was as I feared it would be after Jebbin's report to me. To my, and I'm sure Henry Schneider's, great disappointment, Tracy didn't have much to tell. She couldn't remember anything from Friday with much clarity. She sort of remembered being at crochet class that morning but not any details about what she had done, and she couldn't remember the afternoon session at all. For whatever reason, the only thing she remembered from the whole time she was being held captive were the cowboy clothes. That she had to put them on, that she didn't want to, and that they weren't hers.

She didn't remember anything about who had taken her, the sort of place he—or she—had taken her, or how she had ended up on our front porch.

One more thing she remembered clearly: she thought it was right before she realized she was alone in a bathroom and could take off the cowboy clothes (but of course it had to have been sooner than that) was a voice saying to her, "I'm sorry about all this. You aren't her."

Chapter 7

I WAS JUST THINKING I SHOULD TEXT MADISON WHEN SHE TEX-
ted me.

> *"Listened w/ headphones on. Mom thought was listen-*
> *ing to music. Total washout! 'Cept for that 'You're not her'*
> *bit. Shame didn't use a proper noun instead of pronoun. All*
> *quiet on the homefront. Momma & I crocheting in fam room*
> *watching chick flick."*

I texted back that we'd compare our impressions later and
hoped she and her Mom had a good afternoon. Which made me
wish I had Molly at home to do the same thing with, although
Molly hadn't yet taken to knitting or crocheting, but we sure have

shared many an afternoon or evening watching a chick flick over the years. Yet, I thought and smiled, I really couldn't complain too much. Yes, she wasn't home all the time but she was more than old enough to not be home all the time, and we did see her and Freddy every Friday evening for dinner and a movie. Well, most every Friday. They sometimes had something they went to on the University of Illinois campus or, like last night, they had a snow storm go through Champaign/Urbana that didn't come anywhere close to Twombly, so they stayed put. Just as well with all the stuff going on with Tracy.

Tracy.

I started feeling antsy again just thinking about her. I thanked the Lord that she hadn't been raped, yet she was still going to have to deal with knowing she was kidnapped and not being able to remember anything about it that might help catch the kidnapper.

And the weird thing about the clothes.

What was it with the clothes, other than they were predominately red?

And why all the red things?

And "You're not her." What was with that?

Too many thoughts. I went to the closet, winterized myself, took Sophie's leash off the hook, called her, hooked her up, and we headed out the door. The day had remained dreary with the temperature shifting around between 29° F and 33° F and flurries now floated down like on a charming winter-scene postcard. All the better for me. I don't mind the cold when it's not in the single digits or minus figures and I love an artistic-looking snowfall.

I started for the Ramm Music and Science Garden but, as can easily happen to me when I've too much going on in my head, I ended up at the entrance to the Japanese Garden instead with that uncomfortable feeling that I had no idea how I'd gotten there.

I wasn't sure I wanted to go in, even though Masaki Watanabe, the master gardener for the Japanese Garden, had made major changes in the garden after he and Sophie and I had found Dr. Timothy Law dead in the Hill and Pond (Chisen-Kaiyu-skiki) raked sand part of the garden last June. It was still Chisen-Kaiyu-skiki style, but instead of the raked sand allusion to a body of water, the waterfall coming down the "cliff" now fell into a real pond. The pond emptied into the stream that led through to the Tea Garden (Rojiniwa) where it fed its smaller pond before being recycled back around to the waterfall. Except in the winter. Like most fountains, the waterfall was shut off for the season and the water re-circulated directly back into the pond.

"A great deal of water to wash away the evil of the deed," Masaki had told me. "And koi. Now the koi from the smaller pond and the stream swim here too and bring their good fortune, courage, and perseverance to this part of my garden. And lights. There are underwater lights to clear away the darkness."

And by the end of the summer, when all the changes had been made, Masaki had a Shinto priest come and do a Harae, a purification ceremony, for the entire garden. The ceremony was small, private, and beautiful. Only those of us who had been there that morning when Dr. Law was found had been invited so we could share in the purification.

I looked in through the Hill and Pond garden entrance in the south wall of the enclosed garden.

My breath caught in my throat.

The garden was magical in the muted light and silently falling snow. The new pond was like black glass, impervious to the soft touch of the tiny white flakes. The snow was starting to coat objects, including Jairus Twombly and the bench he was sitting on by the edge of the still, black water. In true Twombly style he knew I was there even though his back was to me.

"Good afternoon, Emory. Sophie. It's been quite a day, hasn't it?"

Sophie and I walked over and sat down. "Yes it has." *In more ways than one,* my thoughts added, with Madison and her recording in mind. Unless the Twombly Touch was back in full gear I doubted Jairus knew about his daughter's ability to be a fly on the wall.

"Has there been any more news?" I added.

"Hmm. I don't think so. I'm sure you know the results of the rape kit, for which we are all immensely grateful."

"Yes, Jebbin told me. It's such a relief."

We went silent. And the garden around us was silent, shielded as it is by its well hidden walls. And the snow fell silently, as snow is wont to fall, unlike its cousin rain.

"There's something amiss with me."

My thoughts had just started to rev up again when he spoke. I knew what he was referring to.

"Your intuition is not working like usual, is it?" The Twombly family gift of sight, of having a knowing of things that had just happened or were about to happen, wasn't as well known to outsiders as their uncanny ability to have things go their way. That was called "The Twombly Touch" and was the stuff of legends in our area. But the intuition was guarded. It had caused problems for the family in their past and they'd learned to keep most knowledge of it to themselves. Jairus had talked to me about it because the same gift runs in my own family and he had encouraged me to embrace it.

I could feel some of his tension leave him as he chuffed out a breath, grinned, and leaned into the back of the bench. "It's only working enough that I figured you already knew. No. It isn't. I don't think it has been for a while but I didn't really notice it until yesterday when I got the call about Tracy's kidnapping. I would normally have known before the call came."

He drew in a deep breath of the brisk air, closed his eyes, and tipped his head way back, staying that way as snowflakes landed and melted upon his face.

"I should have known she'd been taken. I should have known when she showed up and I should have known it was at your front door. But I didn't, and ..." Jairus lowered his chin and opened his eyes to gaze into the black-mirror pond. "Now that I'm aware it's silent, Emory, I'm scared. Scared that it seems to have left me and scared that—no—*more* than scared that I hadn't noticed it was gone."

"Have you any ..."

A soft sound from his coat pocket interrupted me. He pulled out his cell phone, looked at it, and took the call.

"Yes? Yes, I'll be there in a few minutes. No, no trouble at all, you were right to call. Be there soon."

He swiped the call away.

My intuition was working just fine. "Home?" I asked because I knew that's where Resie worked from.

"Yes. My P.A. You've met her, I'm sure. At the college Christmas party at the house if nowhere else."

"I was introduced, but not much more. I didn't even get a chance to speak with her beyond 'Hello, nice to meet you.'"

He was quiet for a moment then muttered, talking to himself instead of me. "Strange, most people have said the same sort of thing." Then he looked at me. "At any rate, I'm off home. Dinner is almost ready to be served and Henri prefers to have us all there when the food is brought to the table."

Sophie and I stood as well. "I can understand that. He wants you eating it when it's at its very best. If I had a chef like Henri, I'd never be late to dinner, or lunch, or breakfast for that matter." I smiled and waved the backs of my hands in his direction. "So shoo. Go on with ya. Enjoy a good dinner and try not to let your gift, or its lack, worry you."

He tightened his lips and gave a curt nod. "I'll do my best. Have a good evening, Emory, and you should be getting home yourself."

I looked at the sky. Its gloom had deepened, causing the underwater lights to come on in the pond. The snowfall was heavier. "Yes, Jairus, I think you're right. Good evening to you as well."

He went out the archway in the north wall. Sophie and I went out the one heading south. I needed to get our dinner going, which wouldn't be anything like what the Twomblys would be getting from their Cordon Bleu trained Chef Henri.

"What do you think, Sophie?" I asked her in the perky, nearly baby-talk, tone we so often use when talking to our pets. Sophie looked up at me in response. "Spaghetti or meatloaf for dinner? Huh, girl? Does my good girl have a preference?"

"Woof." Pause. "Woof, woof."

"Meatloaf! Good choice. Daddy's favorite." It's so easy making decisions with your pets. They say what you want them to.

We walked home across the campus leaving paw prints and footprints in the dusting of snow behind us.

Chapter 8

THE ROOM WAS DARK, BUT THE RED NUMBERS STATED SEV-
en-thirty. I'd gone to bed at eleven o'clock, so I figured it was
now a.m.

What was that quote from *The Glass Menagerie?* A sly grin
graced my lips even in my hypnagogic state.

"I'll rise—but I won't shine."

Not the best way for a good Methodist girl to start a Sunday
morning, I suppose, but it had been a long and strange weekend
and lying late abed sounded rather nice. Barring that, rising but
not having to be perky.

My eyes popped open as an elbow dug into my back.

"Fee the at."

"Huh?" I responded to the noises coming from Jebbin.

"Cat. Feed."

I turned to his side of the bed. Kumquat was standing on his chest with her whiskers tickling his face. Gotta love the wonderful feline species. They always seem to know who will be the easiest to annoy. Jebbin had come home after I'd gone to bed, so obviously he was the one with the least amount of sleep.

"Come on, you orange menace." I got up and she jumped down and ran for our bathroom where she was joined by Hortense and Sophie. I haven't been alone in the bathroom first thing in the morning for years. After taking care of things in there, the gang and I headed for the kitchen where Sophie would get let out while I fixed all the four-footed kids their breakfasts.

The forecast hadn't said anything about the snow that had started yesterday, well, at least not about any accumulation.

The forecast had been wrong.

Not that Sophie minded; she loves playing in snow and she tippy-toed down the stairs before bounding out into at least a foot of white diamond flakes sparkling in the glow of the yard light that shone over the small deck with the stairs down to the backyard. I stood inside the now glassed-in porch and watched her romp for a few minutes before nature's call forced her to interrupt her frolicking, then I turned back into the house to fix everyone's food.

I made the decision that my man and I would skip church today, asking the Lord's understanding as I did so. It's an awkward decision for the daughter of a retired Methodist minister, but there are times I feel it's the right thing to do. Jebbin and I hadn't had much ... together time of late and what with how crazy the last two days had been and the foot of snow on the ground I figured—why not? And so we spent a leisurely morning being ...

companionable, then having a lovely breakfast off TV trays in the family room by the fireplace while watching the Cecil B. DeMille version of *The Ten Commandments* on DVD to sort of make up for missing church. Later, while we were having a banjo and fiddle bluegrass gospel jam session, my cell phone rang.

"Hel …"

"You need to come over now. I need you now."

I barely recognized Amy Twombly's agitated voice. Visions of some sort of domestic violence were jumping into my head.

"Amy. What's the matter? Why do you need *me?*" I looked at a clock—it was 2:40 p.m.

"It's this damn … darn crocheting. I've gotten it all messed up somehow. Yes, that's what it is, the crocheting. I need you to come right now to show me what to do because … I just need you to."

"Ah … well … um, can't Madison help you wi—"

"Ah, ha! Yes, of course you'd suggest Madison. My daughter. *My* daughter. Of course you'd know about what *my* daughter knows. Everyb-bod-body kn-knows abou-about Madison e-except me." Amy's words got lost in her sobs.

"Ah." What should I say? "Ah. Amy?"

A tiny, itty-bitty "Yes?" came in reply.

"Do you really want me to come over?"

A minuscule "Yes." Then a pause. Then a "'Scuse me."

For a moment I heard nose blowing and sniffing at a distance, then Amy was back.

"Please, Emory. I … I'm sorry I, ah, went off on you." She actually sounded contrite. "I'm, um, I haven't been myself lately and I, actually, Madison said maybe I should, ah, you know, ask you to come. And, ah …"

I could hear Madison in the background now, though I

couldn't understand what she was saying.

"She says you should come and bring your crocheting and your dog, Sloopie."

More off-phone talking.

"Sophie. Your dog Sophie. Will you come?"

I knew the snowplows had been out, Twombly has excellent road crews. They would have salted all the intersections too. I looked at my warm husband and the glowing fire. Drat.

"Yes. I'm happy to come and bring my crocheting and Sophie. Will twenty minutes be soon enough? We haven't blown out our driveway yet."

Relief gushed out with her "Yes!"

We said goodbye and I explained the call to Jebbin. He agreed it was weird but also agreed I should go. We both got dressed and then Jebbin went out to blow out the drive while I gathered up my stuff and wondered what my tingly gettin'-a-knowin' feeling was trying to tell me, but I hadn't a clue.

I parked my little yellow Beetle in the circle drive of the Twombly mansion, or estate, or … well, it's a big house. Not like most of us think of a mansion, it doesn't take up a city block or two and doesn't have more wings than a flock of geese, but it's a lovely large home. Centered on a rise in the midst of two acres of mown yard, it's a red brick Italianate-style house with white trim, facing north, with two high-ceilinged floors for the entire main house. What used to be the winter kitchen is in a one-storey wing off the south-west corner with a short breezeway off that leading to the former summer kitchen, which is well shaded by large old oak trees on its east, south, and west sides. The summer kitchen is now the fami-ly video games and home theater room since, with improvements to the house's insulation, there is no longer a need for a summer kitchen. The front porch spans the entire width of the home with the west end of it screened in and a door into that from what was, in the day, the informal parlor but is now called the family room. The attic is more a third floor filled with the servants' rooms and some storerooms. Lovely oval-shaped windows under the eaves let light into those rooms and, of course these days, the entire area is well insulated and air-conditioned, though it must have been brutally hot in the old days.

The family still has live-in help: Iga, the full-time housekeeper and Henri, the full-time chef. When Cora, Jam VII, and Madison were little, there was also a live-in "mother's helper". Not a full-time nanny—the Twomblys never went in for nannies, feeling that it was best for the children and the parents if they interacted with each other as much as possible—the mother's helper was just that. Mom did most of the care while the mother's helper gave the mother a chance to take naps and do the entertaining expected of a rich man's wife.

Iga opened the door in response to my knock and escorted me into the family room.

"Ms. Amy will be with you shortly," was all she said before turning on her heels and shutting the door to the entry hall behind her. I was caught off guard by her coolness. I've been to enough events at the Twomblys' that Iga usually greeted me in a friendlier manner. The tension in the home wasn't just affecting the family. As soon as the door clicked shut, Madison popped out of a high-wingback chair facing the fireplace where a cozy fire was contentedly burning.

"Hi, Emory!" She hurried over to grab my arm and pull me toward the fireplace. "Iga didn't know I was in here. She thinks it's just going to be you and Mom and Sophie. She would probably have whooshed me out of here had she seen me. Have a seat."

She waved me toward the loveseat between the chair she'd been in and a matching chair on the other side of the grouping. I saw what I recognized as her mother's crocheting spread across the seat of the small sofa and I hesitated to sit down.

Madison shoved all her mother's things to the end nearest the chair she'd been in, then sat back down. "Mom will want to sit between us, I think. Just make yourself comfy at that end."

I placed my yarn caddy with my crocheting in it next to a small bottle with a paper label saying "olive oil" on the end table between my end of the loveseat and the other wingback chair before sitting down.

"Mama's the one needing some help," Madison continued, "so I figured you two should sit next to each other." She looked around. "Where's Sophie?"

"For some reason, known only to her, she didn't want to come. I'm sorry," I said.

"It's okay. I just thought it might be good for Mom to have someone to pet." Madison bent down, reached under her chair, and pulled out a well loved, stuffed ... something with a bulbous nose. Its brown fur was faded and matted, the foot-and-a-half-long torso was almost pancake flat, the painted eyes on pieces of flat oval plastic were partially worn off. She caught my quizzical expression, hugged the critter, and smiled. "Emory, meet Mr. Moose. My dearest old stuffed animal. His antlers fell off ages ago. Iga stitched the holes closed so he wouldn't leak his stuffing. They'd been mended before but the last time the corduroy they were made from was so threadbare there was no way to stitch them back on." She paused, a look of bemused, sentimental embarrassment on her young face. "I've kept them, they're on the shelf behind where he usually sits in my room."

I reached over to shake his arm. "Nice to meet you, Mr. Moose. Our Molly still has Kitty, her very first stuffed animal. Kitty went to University of Illinois with her last fall. I still had my old worn out Humpty Dumpty pillow doll when I got married."

With a nod of understanding to me and final squeeze to Mr. Moose, she tucked him back under the chair. "I'll pull him out for Mom if she needs him."

I'd never been in this room of the house and I could see why; like in the old days, this was a relaxed place for the family, not for visitors. Although the formal parlor, where parties were held, and the dining room had all the original furniture in them, the informal parlor/family room had what most of us modern folk like to sit on. What had looked from the back like traditional wing-back chairs were actually cushier models that were also recliners. The loveseat was a camelback style but the cushions were soft and inviting. There was a moderate-sized flat-screen TV over the mantelpiece. I was just about to say something when the sound of raised voices came from somewhere off to my left. We both looked toward the sounds.

"Um … that's the dining room," Madison said softly. She listened a moment. "It's Mom and Resie, I think. Henri's the only guy in the house and it's definitely not him, and it doesn't sound like Iga either."

"I wish we could understand them." I turned to look at Madison as a thud vibrated the floor and a crash reverberated through the walls and doors. "You don't happen to have the dining room bugged, do you?"

She didn't lighten up as I thought she might, but merely shook her head and gazed anxiously at the pair of pocket doors that separated the two rooms. They parted at that moment as Amy Twombly charged into the room.

"That conniving little bitch!" She paused to turn and slam the doors back together, then leaned her head against them. "She's wicked and evil and a menace and … and … I'm putting an end to her plots no matter what it takes!" Amy pounded her fist into the door. There was another pause, then … "Madison?"

"Yes, Mom?"

"Is Emory here?"

"Yes."

Amy lifted her head off the dark wood of the doors, raised her shoulders then let them drop as she took a deep, noisy breath before turning around. The attempt at a smile that marred her features was frightful.

"Thank you for coming, Emory." She walked over to an iPod set in the dock of a speaker system, and a moment later "Cherish" by The Association filled the room at a nice background music volume—noticeable but we wouldn't have to shout to hear each other talk. She stood there through the first verse of the song, eyes closed, softly singing along, then came over and sat primly in the empty chair instead of on the loveseat beside me. "If the music is too loud, let me know. I need to calm down before we work on crocheting, and light rock usually helps. I hope this hasn't ruined any plans you and, ah … what's his … Oh yes, Jebbin might have had."

"No, not really. We'd watched a movie earlier and were having a little bluegrass jam session, just the two of us, when you called. No problem at all."

"Good. Good. I'm, ah, sure you heard some of that." She gestured toward the dining room like a marionette with an amateur working its strings. "Those doors are thick but not sound proof."

"Only enough to hear it was an argument, Mom," Madison interjected.

"Hmm. Well, that's … ah … that's good. No need for you and Emory to have to know all the gory details."

Amy had been looking all around the room like a gawker in a new place. Now she looked back and forth between her daughter and me.

"Could you hear … ? Ah, could you tell who … ?"

"No," I replied. "We couldn't understand but Madison thought you were talking to Resie."

Amy's pale face went pink. Her jaw muscles tightened.

"Yes. Yes I was talking to Resie. Dear, wonderful, efficient PA, organized, intruding, conniving …" The pink faded from her face. Her eyes glinted. "She backed into a display stand, banged it hard against the wall, and then the whole thing fell over sideways. The vase on it was a gift to me from Jairus' mother back when Jairus and I were newlyweds. It smashed to bits, of course." Amy looked at her daughter. "I'm sorry, Maddy, the lovely flowers you brought home for me yesterday were in the vase. Water and bro …" Her voice grew as sharp as the shards of that broken vase. "Water and broken flowers all over the parquet floor. I told her she da … ah, darn well better clean up the mess she made. Not that *she* cares what she breaks around here. She's already stealing everything *she* cares about! They think I don't notice … No! Jairus thinks I don't even care about what's going on around here. But I know. I *know*! She's thinking I'll leave but she doesn't know who she's backed into a corner." She then glared at me. "You all think I'm some horrible bitch; yes, you think I'm a horrible bitch." Her gaze flicked between me and her daughter. "But you ain't seen nothing yet! I made my first move and she's the loser."

I was in shock. I couldn't see Madison but I had the feeling that she wasn't doing much better. Amy reached over and grabbed a handful of tissues out of a lovely stained glass tissue box on the end table that sat between us and jammed her face into them.

"She can't have you, Maddy. She can't have you, or Cora, or Jam VII. And she can't have your Papa, unless …"

For several minutes we all sat there, Amy loudly sobbing, Madison sniffling, and me wondering what on earth I was doing here and why did Sophie's doggie intuition let her know to stay home while mine hadn't tried hard enough to keep me there.

Amy got up, tossed the tissues into a trash basket on the near end of the fireplace hearth.

"Enough." She marched over to the end of the loveseat by her daughter, pushed her crocheting things to the middle of the seat, plopped herself down then reached over to pat Madison's arm. "Enough of that. As I said, I made my move." Amy sniffed hard and, very unlike her usual self, ran her right sleeve under her nose before looking over at me. "I asked you here for crocheting help, not to listen to me air the family business."

I opened up my yarn caddy. I didn't know what else to do, even though I didn't think she was in any condition to deal with a problem with her crocheting. "Yep, that you did, and I'm all ready to help you out." I pulled out my hook, threaded the end of the yarn through the hole in the lid of the caddy, and then clicked it closed. "What are you needing help with?"

Amy had already picked up her work. It was a triangle; she obviously hadn't decided how wide to make the afghan so there wasn't a second corner. The two outside edges were about two feet long with the jagged edged "inside" of the piece being twice that.

She had chosen yarn made from the herd at Prairie Rose Alpacas, an alpaca farm in Golden County, in a soft peach, a sandy beige, natural off white, and a pale sea-greenish blue for her afghan. She had made quite a show of telling the class that, as a Twombly, she felt it was important that she support businesses in their area.

She stood up and moved her supplies around on the seat, then started to pick them all up. "Well doesn't this just top it all off! Where's my hook? I'm not losing that hook." She started sniffing again. "I like that hook. It's a pretty hook and it's classy looking and ..."

She dropped everything back on the sofa and headed for the dining room doors.

"I had it in my hand when I went in here."

I felt as if a hundred or so rabbits had run over my grave, causing me to shudder. *Don't go in there!* the knowing screamed in my head.

"Amy," I stood up in my anxiousness. "I'll lend you one of mine. You're using an F size hook, aren't you? I brought one."

"Thanks, but no. I want my Furls hook."

She parted the doors and went in.

"Oh my God!"

I had just taken a step toward the dining room but now I was running toward it with Madison close behind me. I went in on the right side of the table, Madison went to the left toward her mom at the far end.

"Get it out! Get it out! Get it out!"

Amy was screaming the words over and over, hands held to either side of her face like Edvard Munch's painting *The Scream*.

There was a body on the floor at the far end of the table on my side. I heard doors sliding. I swung my head to look at the doors into the main hall.

"What on earth is …"

"Iga," I yelled to be heard above Amy's hysterics. "Get Amy and Madison out of here, now!"

I heard her rounding up the two Twomblys and taking them somewhere else. My attention was on the body on the floor.

A couple of steps closer and I could see what Amy was scream-ing about. There lay the display pedestal surrounded by mangled flowers and a porcelain vase in shards, some of which were resting in the blood on the floor as it bled into the water the flowers had been in. Despite knowing there had been an argument in here a short while before, despite the overturned furniture and broken vase that could have been knocked over for a very different reason than the one Amy gave us, and even though Amy's Bloodwood cro-chet hook was protruding from Resie's left eye, I knew with every shiver running through my soul that Amy hadn't done this. And, since Resie wasn't writhing in agony, I also knew she was dead.

Chapter 9

"I SO NEED THIS, HON," I SIGHED.

I was cuddled up with Jebbin on the couch in the family room. A low fire burned gently on the grate, we were both in our jammies and the dirty dishes from two grilled cheese sandwiches and hot cocoa sat on TV trays. Kumquat was next to me, Hortense was next to Jebbin, and Sophie was on the floor between us and the fireplace. A cozy, homey moment … except for the fact I'd spent the last part of the afternoon and all of Sunday night at the Golden County Sheriff's Department being fingerprinted, waiting to be questioned, and being questioned.

The grandfather clock beside the stairs chimed and tolled once.

"That dratted Henry Schneider!" I pulled away from Jebbin's

side so I could look at him while I talked. "I'm sorry. I guess I'm just not ready to relax. He's going to drag everything out as much as he can. Just gonna make the most of this being in his jurisdiction and not the city of Twombly's, and that Jairus isn't going to be able to ply the Twombly Touch as usual, since his wife is the prime suspect."

"I know," Jebbin sympathized. "He tried to send the whole case off to the state labs, until they told him how backed up they are and why didn't he just use the fully licensed and accredited lab here at the college, since it *is* the official lab for the county. I know 'cause they called me and told me they did. Personally, I don't think they like Henry any more than we do and just didn't want to put up with him."

"And he made poor Madison sit by herself in an interrogation room while Simone Bogardus, you know, the Twombly family lawyer, was busy watching out for Amy while they questioned her." I huffed. "Henry said he didn't want us talking to each other but he also didn't want all the 'BS', as he put it, that would get thrown around if he put a minor girl in a cell just to hold her for questioning."

"He said he's insisting on an outside forensic expert to duplicate every test I run and there'll be a deputy in the lab with us at all times keeping an eye on us. Gonna do the same to Antonia in her pathology lab. Henry better make sure that one has a strong stomach." Jebbin shook his head. "I just love being watched while I work. And I sure hope he gets Chatty to help. Jim from up Chicago way is alright, good scientist and all, just not as congenial to work with."

"But he sure didn't mind putting *me* in a cell. I mean, really? I arrived while Amy was already in the dining room with Resie and didn't go in there myself until Amy had gone back in and found her on the floor." I stared at the fire and trembled. "It was … It was like something out of some low budget horror film. Surreal. Like it had been staged. Then it was all too real and I had run back into the family room, which was empty because Iga had had the good sense not to take Amy and Madison in there with the connecting doors still open. Then I went out into the hall and could hear Amy crying from the direction of the formal parlor. Iga had taken them in there and had been just wrapping an afghan around Amy's shoulders when I had stumbled in."

I shivered again and Jebbin pulled me back to his side, with his arm around my shoulders.

"Thank you." I sighed then continued a little more calmly. "What a mess. What a hideous, terrible thing. Amy kept whimpering. Madison looked ready to pass out. I was cold and numb. None of us said much of anything, we all sat there. Except Iga, she went and checked on Henri." I looked over at Jebbin. "You know, the Twombly's chef." He nodded and I went on. "I just remembered. He poked his head out of the kitchen just as Iga was rounding up Amy and Madison. I vaguely remember looking up when I heard him gasp, 'Oh my God!' before I went back to checking out what had happened and who was on the floor."

I went quiet for a moment as a tiny little quiver prickled the back of my neck. Not quite like when I get one of my insights … and yet like that feeling.

"Where was I? Oh, yeah. In the living room with Amy and Madison. Then that blasted Henry Schneider showed up! He was snide and condescending. Almost gloating that this had happened to the Twomblys. And then, I just know he waited till last to interview me at the station. And he kept Amy locked up. Didn't even offer to let her go home with one of those tracking ankle bracelets. I overheard one of the deputies saying Henry told her she'd just have to wait till Monday morning, like any other murderer, for bail to be set. She didn't do it, though. I'd swear Amy didn't do it."

"You think she's being set up?"

"I don't know. No, I've no idea at all, I just …" Jebbin doesn't really know that much about my gift, other than I have strong intuition and often "guess" right about things. I wasn't going to make an issue of it now. "I just have a feeling that she didn't do it."

He nodded, then there was silence.

The furry kids had slept through it all.

"That fancy crochet hook, huh?" Jebbin asked after we'd spent time thinking our own thoughts.

"Yeah. More's the pity. It's such a nice hook and I'm sure Amy will never want to touch it again—if it ever gets taken out of evidence storage." I thought a moment. "Does stuff ever get taken out of evidence storage?"

"Yes … And no."

I waited but he didn't continue. Then he grinned.

"You're havin' me on." I mock pouted.

"Not really," he said, patting my hand. "Often, there aren't hard and fast rules about it, and seeing as in big cities stored evidence builds up pretty quickly, there's often a need to get rid of it, usually by incineration. They even melt down guns and knives. That said, some of the big cities are the ones that keep it pretty much forever because they have more storage space."

"So, no 'Cold Case Files' in tiny town, USA?"

We laughed together before he answered, "Yes and no." He held up his free hand. "No. Really. Not just being cute again. It really depends on the attitude of the officials in the town, if they feel they have a place to store the stuff adequately and if they truly might need it again."

"Stored so it doesn't get damaged, you mean?"

"Exactly. Some evidence will keep for ages in almost any conditions—well, reasonably dry I should say. Reasonably dry conditions. Few things will mess stuff up more than moisture. Often, dried up stuff can be rehydrated so it can still be usable, former bodily fluids and body parts for instance, but moisture normally means things will mold and rot. So, yeah. The conditions you have for mass storage makes a difference."

I nodded. "Either way, I doubt she'd ever touch that hook again." A little shiver ran up my back and I added. "Don't think I would, either."

Jebbin reached over and rubbed my shoulder. "Ready for bed?" he asked after a few minutes.

"Yeah, I think I finally am. I'll get up early tomorrow and text my students to find out if they want to have crochet class. Sometimes routine is a comfort; that and it'll give us a time and place to talk about it all."

He nodded, giving my shoulder a final squeeze. "Sounds like a plan."

He picked up the dishes. I followed behind him shutting off the lights and we climbed the stairs toward the main floor and our bedroom.

Chapter 10

"THE SITUATION YESTERDAY AFTERNOON WAS TRAGIC."

Sheriff Sammy Watkins had on his stern yet sympathetic face as Jebbin and I watched him making the first official statement about Resie (actually Theresie) Schmid's murder on the early, early edition of the Twombly and Golden County news; 5:30 a.m. on our local cable channel, WTGC-TV. Broad shouldered, and blond haired, the cameraman's close headshot of our handsome sheriff easily filled the screen.

"The cause of Theresie Schmid's death was a wooden crochet hook that penetrated her skull behind her left eye." He read from the cards in his hand 'cause Lord only knows he most likely couldn't remember what he was supposed to say well enough to not say something he oughtn't. He wasn't stupid, just vocally awkward.

"At least someone came up with a less gross way to describe …"

"Shhh!" Jebbin cut me off.

I really should have known to wait until the interview was over. Any official comments in the media were important to Jebbin. He liked to know the publicly declared official stance on any case he had to deal with.

"At this time," Sammy on the TV continued, "we did make an arrest and we have our suspect in custody awaiting a bail hearing, which is scheduled to take place at seven o'clock this morning at the Golden County Courthouse."

"Who are you holding?"

"Who's your suspect?"

"Is it a Twombly?"

The reporters did their usual question barrage. Sammy held one of his large, well-muscled hands up for quiet.

"We have been holding Amy Susannah Twombly in custody since around ten o'clock last night."

The reporters went nuts. You could barely hear Sammy say he'd take no more questions at this time before he strode back into the county courthouse. The Sheriff's Department took up the entire basement level of the building and then some, having been extended (still underground) in the 1980s. It worked well to have their facilities be part of the courthouse since they had the primary responsibility for escorting defendants to and from the courtrooms on the third floor.

I aimed the clicker and shut the small TV in the kitchen off.

"You were saying?" Jebbin took a drink of his coffee. This morning he was using his coffee mug that has the structural formula of a caffeine molecule on one side with "If you can read this …" written under it and "Thank a chemistry teacher" on the reverse side.

"I was just saying that 'penetrating her skull behind her left eye' was a better way to describe what happened than a lot of other ways I can think of."

"I'm sure you can. You didn't sleep well last night."

"No, I didn't." I was having chamomile tea this morning for just that reason. I was still feeling grumpy and edgy, and I reached for my cell phone. "I'm gonna text the crochet class students. I'll just say if they want to come that's good with me and if no one shows I'll understand that too."

I started my message then stopped.

"What's happening with you?" I asked Jebbin. "Have you heard anything yet? Wait. Stupid question. I would have heard your phone if you had. I'm just not all here today."

"It's okay, Hon. I haven't but I'm gonna head on over to the lab anyway. There's always something to do and I reckon I'll be getting a call at some point in the morning. I'm sure Antonia has started her autopsy by now, or will be soon and we probably ..."

His phone rang. He grunted a few affirmative sounding grunts then said, "See you there in half an hour. I've only had one cup of coffee and no breakfast yet and I'm not diving into this mess on an empty stomach."

Irritable noises came through the phone.

Jebbin said sternly, "Live with it, Henry. Half an hour," and then disconnected the call.

"Well," I said, "there we go. The answer to that question. I'll get some oatmeal going and some scrambled eggs. That'll stick with you for a while."

"Thanks, Sweetie. Got some good news that I didn't react to 'cause I didn't want to let Henry know that it's good news. They're bringing in Chatty for the second forensics guy."

"Will he be here for dinner?"

Jebbin drained his coffee mug then set it down. "I'll let you know when I know. I'm off to get dressed. Refill that when ya get a chance and holler when breakfast is on the table." He gave me a quick kiss then headed to our bedroom.

I finished my text, sent it to the class, and started on our meal.

"Meow!" Hortense insisted as I heard Sophie scratch at the door and give a polite "Wuff!" to be let in.

Okay. I fed the critters *then* started on our meal.

Everyone showed up for class, except Amy and Madison, but we all expected that. Everyone asked if I knew anything. Students didn't usually listen to the local news, except for the local commuter students, because they grew up here and know most of the people the news talks about, or political science majors who were required to for their classes.

But it was now past nine o'clock, the campus is a rather small community within a rather modest sized town, and everyone knew who had been arrested.

"Well," I said, "Dr. Crawford got a call before breakfast from Captain Henry Schneider of the Sheriff's Department letting him know the lab here on campus will be doing the forensic work and that everything will be done by him and a second, independent forensic scientist with a sheriff's deputy observing at all times."

"They're letting them work on it here, with the Twomblys being in charge of ... well, everything around here?" Ed Ramsey pulled his striped green, yellow, and white Twombly College colors afghan out of his green and yellow Twombly College duffel bag.

"It is the official lab for Golden County. The state lab requested they use it since they are backlogged, as usual, and it's a completely licensed, certified, and whatever else is needed, lab that the county uses in every other situation. However, Ed, that's why there will be the second forensic scientist and the watchful deputy."

"What's happening with Amy? How is Madison, do you know?"

I almost didn't hear Tracy's questions. To be honest, I was surprised she was here. The hospital had released her Sunday afternoon and I think we had all been surprised that she had stayed on campus instead of going home with her mother and grandmother.

"I … I can sort of relate to …" Tracy continued, struggling with her emotions, eyes fixed on her clenched hands that pushed into her thighs more than rested on her lap. "Even though it isn't the same sort of crime, well … I know they both have to be really scared. I mean, I'm scared, staying here at school, but I decided scary things happen everywhere and I like my teachers and my friends here."

Her right hand disentangled from her left to grab at Suzanne's left hand that was resting on the couch between them. They held on tight.

The image wavered as I teared up. "I—we're—glad you've stayed, Tracy. Ah, well, I haven't talked to the family yet, so …"

My cell phone rang.

I usually had it off and would leave it upstairs during class, just as the students were required to have their phones off, but I had explained to the class that I was making an exception since my husband was working on the case and someone from the Twombly family might call and I reckoned we'd all want to know whatever we could.

The screen on my phone read, "Jairus."

"Hello."

"Hello, Emory." His voice was a ghost of its usual depth and confidence. "Did anyone … Is your class meeting?"

I looked around at the anxious faces of my students, my friends. "Yes." The circle of faces perked up without losing any of their tension. "Everyone is here."

"Tell them it's me and put me on speaker, please."

I complied and set the phone on the coffee table in front of the couch.

"Good morning to you all."

Everyone "good morning-ed" in reply.

"First I wanted to say that I'm glad you all decided to attend your crocheting class: that you are carrying on. Ah, secondly, I wish for you all to know, if you don't already, that my personal assistant was … uh … killed yesterday afternoon and that my … my wife, Amy, was arrested. Excuse me a moment, please."

While muffled speaking issued from my phone we all looked at each other, suddenly awkward with the distant presence of Amy's husband and Madison's father.

"I'm back. Madison came in and, ah, realized I was talking to you all and she'd like to speak to you. I'll put my phone on speaker."

"Hi," came from another ghostly voiced Twombly. "I wanted to … let you all know that, ah, my Momma is …" Madison stopped, sniffed, blew her nose and, aside to her Father said, "I'm okay, Papa," before addressing us again. "My Momma is under house arrest. Ah, she … um, can't go much of anywhere and I want to stay with her, so … ah, we're staying at the guest house just off campus in Polaris Fields and … um, Emory?"

"Yes, Madison?"

"Would it be okay if we had class here tomorrow? I don't know …"

We heard a sniffy, gaspy, shaky intake of air. "Don't know if Mama will, you know, ah, want to come down and join in, but I'd really like to see you all and be in class and there's plenty of room here and there's a fireplace and everything and Henri can make us lunch." Her words whooshed out of her, escaping before she lost the nerve to finish her request.

I looked around the group seeing their answers in their body language before I asked, but I asked anyway for Madison's benefit. "What do you think, everyone? Henri is a fabulous chef."

"Like the food makes the difference," Tom grinned. "Yeah, Madison. Ed and I are in."

"If Emory is willing to drive us in her Bug, I'll be there, too," Marge said, then laughed, wheezed, coughed, and laughed again. "That was in case you forgot why I'll need a ride to go across campus, Madison."

"Glad you'll come, Marge." The girl's voice was stronger now. "Henri makes this really good soothing tea for congestion. I'll make sure he knows you'll need some."

"We're coming too!" Carrie, Naomi, and Suzanne said in unison.

"And me too, Madison. This is Tracy and I'll be there too."

There was a small pause and when Madison answered I could hear the tears in her voice. "Oh wow! I'm glad you're still in the class, Tracy. That's just … Wow. I knew they'd released you and was hoping you weren't leaving. Cool! Ah," she sniffed. "Okay. I'll see you all for class at nine a.m. here at Cornelia House."

Jairus then thanked us and they said their goodbyes before disconnecting.

Chapter 11

CLASS WENT FINE AFTER JAIRUS' AND MADISON'S PHONE CALL. Everyone worked on their projects and talked about what classes they were going to be taking in the regular semester, how various Twombly teams were doing, and what they had done over Christmas break. Anything, really, except murder and kidnapping.

Tracy wasn't working on the Twombly colors scarf she'd started on.

"You're working on something different, Tracy," Carrie said as Tracy pulled out a skein of Caron brand Simply Soft yarn in a soft peach color. "What'cha going to be making? Did you finish your scarf?"

"No, I didn't finish the scarf. I might do that over the summer or something. I … well, I told Mom and Grandma about the class." She kept her eyes fixed on the yarn in her hands. "I mean, they kinda wondered why I showed up at Emory's house." She didn't go into any more detail than that; we all knew what she was talking about. "They asked if I'd teach them how to do the pattern and I said sure. They left to get dinner, and when they came back to … you know, to the hospital … ah, they had talked to Suzanne and she showed them what she was doing and they bought a bunch of this lovely soft yarn in all these pretty colors and asked if it would be okay if we all worked on an afghan for me, in squares like Suzanne's." She looked up at last, a sort of fragile smile on her face that made me realize just how hard it was for her to talk about this. "That way, I'd have something from them to wrap up in. You know, like they're hugging me when I'm here and they're home. I said, 'Wow! Sure!' and Suzanne suggested we do larger squares than hers and it would get done quicker."

She dug into her tote bag and pulled up several squares in various pastel colors. Her smile looked a little better now and I breathed a sigh of relief as she laid them out for everybody to admire.

"We started while I was still in the hospital and we all worked on them yesterday afternoon and evening while I was with them in their hotel room. I'm staying with them till they go back home, Wednesday afternoon. That was all the time they could get off work." She paused to look at Suzanne. "I'm sure we'll do some more tonight while we watch TV. Suzanne is joining us till Mom and Gram leave."

Tracy and Suzanne giggled. "Yep, a grown up girl sleepover." Suzanne grinned. "Then Tracy will be back in our dorm room."

We all applauded the joint afghan and extended sleepover idea.

There was really a nice variety of projects in the group. Ed was making a Twombly colors afghan for himself. Tom was making a Twombly-colored child-sized afghan for his new nephew who was due to be born in March, then he was going to make himself a Twombly scarf. Carrie was leaving her work in large triangles as shawls for her mother and sisters. My neighbor, Myrtle, was making her very first ever—as in she'd never even owned one before—afghan with Caron Simply Soft in pastel Twombly colors. Suzanne's afghan was going to be made of four-inch squares in rainbow colors, blending from pastel to bold—the oils and acrylics painter in her was showing through. Naomi was making a rectangular shawl for Aine, whose apartment over her shop was always chilly in the winter.

Me, I'm making an afghan for Freddy Wilkinson, my daughter's boyfriend. They're both at University of Illinois working on their masters degrees, so I'm making it in U of I colors: dark blue and orange. Molly took her Twombly green and gold afghan with her—the one I made for her when she started at Twombly for her bachelor's degree—so she didn't need another afghan.

I wondered suddenly what would happen to Madison's scarf, if she'd want to finish it or start something new, like Tracy was doing. I doubted Amy would want to do any more crocheting at all. But, I decided just then, that I'd go buy her a size F bamboo hook and take it with me to Cornelia House, just in case. I'd get a normal, straight-shafted crochet hook that wouldn't look a thing like her ruined Furls hook.

Class time flew by. We had our lunch break, pizza I ordered in from Domino's. Jebbin called during lunch to say that Chatty would be coming for dinner.

"Oh," Jebbin informed me, "Chatty eats beef now."

"Really? How'd that happen?"

"He read that in different parts of India Hindus eat differently and that not all Hindus abstain from beef. Although, he says that buffalo and yak, which are sort of beef-like, are more commonly consumed than cattle."

I'll admit, I was puzzled. "He just now learned that?"

Jebbin laughed. "Yep. He says he's learned more about Hinduism since leaving India than he knew while living there. He said you sort of learn your own region's practices and don't bother with anyone else's. Anyway, he said he was a guest at some client's home and they served beef. He'd recently read about all this and, since he's not that strict a Hindu anyway, decided to not be rude and to try it. He loved it and there you have it."

It was my turn to chuckle. "Well, that will make main course selection a lot easier. How about pork? Dare you ask?"

I heard muffled talking, then—

"Greetings, my dear Emory, and how are you and your class this day? I am sorry for the sorrows you are all facing."

"Greetings, Chatty! My class and I are well, considering all the recent sad and scary events. Thank you for asking."

"I am glad you are all able to uplift each other. The support of community is most important at such times." I could hear his smile right through the phone. "Yes. I eat pork as well. My dearest parents would, I am most certain, be horrified, but I have decided that since I already was not a vegetarian Hindu and since so many Americans eat such a variety of meats, that I would do the same. That said, I do still prefer to have more fish, poultry, and lamb than beef and pork, but I do now eat those meats as well." He paused, a strange sort of pause. "I hope this means you have some new dishes that you can present to me."

I could almost hear him licking his chops in anticipation. The man is such a foodie.

"It does indeed, Chatty! Probably starting tonight, in fact, as all I have in the house right now is beef and ham."

"I look forward to when our supper time arrives. Here is your good husband back."

"What time?" I asked as I heard the phone exchanging hands.

"Seven-ish? Eight-ish?"

"Make it seven-thirty-ish." I was running potential menus through my mind. "See you both then."

Chatty is always so much fun to cook for. I smiled as he helped himself to seconds of the entrée closest to him, then got up to get more from the one at Jebbin's end of the table, rather than interrupt his colleague who was still on his firsts. He truly enjoys and thoroughly compliments even the simplest of dishes. "Hmm … Oh! This, these … what did you call them? Both are wonderful!" He exuded pleasure.

I chuckled at his enthusiasm. "They are Impossible Cheeseburger Pie and, made from the same recipe but with the meat changed, I guess I'd call it Impossible Ham and Cheese Pie. They each have the meat, onions, ah … milk, eggs, salt and pepper, the biscuit mix, of course, and cheese. I used American in the cheeseburger one since people usually use American cheese on cheeseburgers. I used cheddar for the ham and cheese pie. The meat and cheeses were the only difference."

"But each has its own distinct flavor. Impossibly delicious pies, you must mean." He beamed as he dug into his fresh helpings.

"I'm glad you like them so much. I didn't invent them or name them. The recipe booklet says the name is because 'They do the impossible by making their own crust almost like magic.' They're made with a prepackaged dry biscuit mix, and became popular years ago." I had to think about it. "Gosh! Way back in the early 1980s, I think. At any rate, they are really easy to make, filling, and taste good, so I made them quite often when the kids were both at home."

"I will not complain if you were to make more of these while I'm here." Chatty smiled his dazzling smile. What was it about the man that just made me want to please him? At least in a culinary regard. It had to be all the compliments. Not that Jebbin doesn't compliment my cooking, he does, but Chatty just seems to put his whole heart into it.

"I'll do that. I'll also write down the recipes for Deepti and she can make them for you at home."

"Ah!" He nearly clapped his hands. "A true friend of my taste buds."

"So," I began, changing the subject. "What have you two been up to in the lab today?"

The two men looked at each other, then Jebbin sighed in defeat. Chatty obviously wanted to keep eating.

"Oddly enough, things aren't moving along as quickly as we thought they would. Samples from the autopsy are arriving piecemeal from the hospital lab. Various baggies of evidence from the crime scene are doing the same. We've actually had down-time when we've finished with one piece of evidence and end up waiting around for something new to show up." Jebbin shook his head as he helped himself to some more tossed salad. "We got told not to come back tonight, if you can believe that. Specifically, we were told there will be no more evidence coming in tonight."

I felt my brows draw together as my face matched my perplexity. "That's really weird. Usually everyone is in such a hurry that they want everything done yesterday."

No sooner were the words out of my mouth than a thought came into my mind.

"I know that look." Jebbin said, staring at me. "What are you thinking, my little Miss Marple?"

"A rather disturbing thought. Could dear Captain Henry be intentionally slowing things down to aggravate Jairus?"

"I have thought the same thought, Emory." Chatty piped up. He looked back and forth between Jebbin and I, then chose to address his fellow forensic scientist. "I have had such things happen before, although I will admit to wondering if it was just because an independent third party lab was involved. That said, there have been times I have felt as though one agency or the other, or one officer or another, was doing things to purposefully slow us down." He looked back to me. "I have that feeling here, with this case, and with your Captain Henry. He has not shown his face in our lab, but he is the officer in charge of this investigation and yes, the pace of things is abnormally slow for a lab that only serves one low-population county."

I didn't like the sound of this and I was sure the guys didn't like it either.

My voice was tentative. "Obstruction of justice?"

Chapter 12

I THINK WE WERE ALL A BIT IN SHOCK. NORMALLY SUCH A THING would have brought a flurry of discussion, but it didn't. Chatty quietly excused himself to go to his hotel room. He needed to call Deepti, he said.

Jebbin and I got up and cleared the table with the choreographed precision of automatons. He was inside his head and I was in mine, neither one of us comfortable with the words I'd uttered. We didn't like Henry. Henry didn't like us. Henry didn't like the Twomblys. I wasn't sure if it was mutual with Jairus, but it was definitely the case from Henry's side. Even with that, would the captain go so far as to break the law? And why? Was making life more unpleasant than it currently was for the Twombly family that important to Henry? It seemed as though the man had power issues, although I would never have said he had any feelings of incompetency to compensate for.

Then again, *was* Henry breaking the law? Where was the line in the sand that he'd have to cross to make slowing things down a crime?

Lots of questions.

Jebbin and I ended up watching an episode of Margery Allingham's *Campion* on Netflix, then we went to bed.

In the morning we had breakfast and discussed the moving of the crochet class to Cornelia House. We discussed what Jebbin hoped would be available for Chatty and him to work on at the lab. We moved on to the weather prediction from the early, early news: continued cold today; fog tomorrow morning.

"What about Henry?" I finally dared to ask it.

I recognized the glint in Jebbin's eyes. He looked at me the same way I'd seen him look at a troublesome student.

"We are now aware there's a potential issue," he stated in full professorial mode. "Chatty and I will now be looking for anything definitive." His mouth tightened as he drew a deep breath. "I don't suffer cheaters of any ilk, and that really is all there is to say right now." His toughness faded, replaced with a sadness that aged his features. "I hate when this happens in my classes, or in our department, or in our college. But if that's what's going on in this situation, where we're dealing with the law and a life that's been taken … I'll be checking into it on my own. I know officers in other towns in this state. There are people and resources I can get information from, and I will find out just how much he's pullin' the wool over our eyes."

My man is an honest one; not perfect, none of us are, but he is honest and few things drew out his wrath or caused him deeper sorrow than dishonesty in others. Twombly College had expelled more than one student over the years because Dr. Jebbin Crawford would only give a cheater one chance to mend their ways. Not compromising on issues of honesty was one of his characteristics on my long list of things I loved about him.

My dearest went his way and I finished getting ready to go mine. With Hortense and Kumquat begging to play in the water, bumping into my arms, and trying to play with my toothbrush, hairbrush, and dangly earrings, my time in the bathroom counted as my morning calisthenics. I had Freddy's U of I afghan in my tote and was getting into my coat when Marge knocked at the door.

"Good Morning, Emory. Percy asked if I'm leaving home." She nodded toward the pull-a-long suitcase that stood beside her on our porch. "He also asked if I was making my afghan big enough for Aristaeus, the only one of the ancient Greek giants to supposedly survive all the wars against them."

Dr. Percy Purtle was Twombly College's only Classics professor.

I pulled the front door closed behind me and reached for her luggage. "That is one of the drawbacks to making an afghan that is made all in one piece, instead of in pieces like a Granny Square afghan," I said sympathetically. "They get rather large to be hauling around so most people only work on them at home. I'll take the case so you aren't having to try to lift it into the car."

I'd pushed the button to open the garage door before I left the house so I double beeped the car to open both doors then popped the trunk to stash the suitcase. Marge was all buckled in and ready to go, I did the same, backed us out of the garage, closed the door, backed us down the drive, and headed east to the end of the block. Left onto College Avenue, four long city blocks, then another left onto North Star Drive, which is the northern border of the original Twombly College campus, the way our street, Rigel Boulevard, is the border to the south.

Cornelia House is at the western end of North Star Drive. It was not part of the Polaris Fields housing development that was built as faculty housing, as was our development, Orion Fields. Cornelia House has an entire block to itself, just west of the end of Polaris Fields, so that the visiting professors and other special guests of the college would have some space to themselves to relax and not be "on display" for their entire visit. Cornelia house is across North Star Drive from the row of buildings on campus comprised of the Victor Herbert Music Building, the John Dalton Science Building, the J.M. Ramm Music and Science Garden, and the Mary Agnes Yerkes Fine Arts Building.

We were passing by the front part of the campus, where Oglethorpe and Mitchell dormitories are, and nearing the Science building, when a figure came stumbling though the un-shoveled snow of the campus grounds between the Music and Fine Arts buildings.

"Look!" Marge flapped her hand at the windshield. "Someone's not looking well balanced. Student you think, Emory? Wrong night for a kegger. Watch out!" She gasped.

The figure had careened across the eastbound street of the boulevard, covered the island in two strides and now took an off-balance dive into my lane.

I couldn't slam on my brakes.

The street was plowed but still icy.

I down shifted while frantically tapping my brakes and steering toward the right-hand curb, praying that I'd miss the person now spread-eagled on the slick asphalt.

Chapter 13

I FELT NO THUMP-THUMP THROUGH THE STEERING WHEEL. Thank God! I must have missed him.

"Got your pho …?"

"Dialing." Marge was poking like mad at the cell phone in her hand. "Go check on him."

We had skidded clear past the figure on the street, who had not moved as far as I could tell. Whoever it was, was tall, dressed in heavy, work-grade bib-overalls that had what looked like soot or scorch marks on them. The mousy grey-brown hair bundled at the nape of the neck into a tidy bun, along with the outfit, told me she was Lilly Rose Comfort, one of Twombly College's sculpture professors who worked in welded metals. She, not a he. With a groan, Lilly started to push herself up from the slushy pavement.

"Hi, Lilly." I leaned down beside her. "It's Emory Crawford. You might better lay still, Hon."

"An' leave … mah … mah what's-it … mah face." Her Alabama drawl didn't help her slurred speech. "Cain't leave mah face in the … wa-et … slush."

"Ah, no. I'll … ah, get ya something, Lilly. Just don't move," I drawled in response to her accent.

A green, yellow, and white pastel fluffy object appeared in front of my face.

"Use this."

I looked up at Marge, then back at what she was holding out to me, then back at her. It was her unfinished afghan—her crochet hook still woven into one side of it so it wouldn't get lost.

She shrugged. "It's acrylic. It's washable."

"Thanks." I nodded to her as I took the folded fabric. "Let me lift your head a bit, Lilly, an' I'll tuck this in so your face is off the snow."

"Mmm. Yeah. Snow. Don't get no snow down home. No snow. No … Where's he?"

She started squirming to lift up again.

"Who?" I asked, holding her down as gently as I could. Sirens approaching in the distance carried well on the crisp air.

"Him. Kid with … mah coffee. Coffee from … from Fill … Fill … coffee shop place."

The sirens were getting close. I didn't have much time to talk to her.

"Fill Your Cup. You ordered coffee, Lilly?"

"Yeah. Mah coffee. They … they send mah coffee to studio."

"You have a standing order?"

"Yep ... Mah coffee ... Old order. New young'n."

"You didn't know the delivery boy?"

"No. 'Twasn't ... Charlie ... New young'n ... Tall boy."

She was talking slower now, or maybe it was just because I wanted her to hurry.

"Towhead," she dragged on. "But brows ... too dark. Clean lines ... edges ... ta his face. Good ta sculpt ... Weird. He ... talked ... weird stuff ... Ah felt weird ... Ah feel weird ... Coffee was so ... purdy."

"Your coffee was pretty, Lilly?"

"Ah-huh ... had purdy red bow." She took a deeper breath. "Ah needed fresh ... breath. Too close. Boy ... crowded me. Shoved him. Ran."

A soft sigh escaped Lilly as she passed out.

Marge leaned down to talk into my ear rather than shout over the sirens. "Red bow on her coffee cup?"

We looked at each other.

"Tracy." We said in unison.

The EMTs checked Lilly out, rolled her onto a spinal board and loaded her up in the ambulance as soon as they could, to get her out of the cold. A couple of campus security guys showed up, and a Twombly city police squad car showed up. No sheriff's cars though, for which I, at least, was grateful. I'd almost hit Lilly, Marge had called the situation in, so we were questioned by everyone who had cause to question us. The sirens and lights had attracted a crowd, which included the crochet class, including Madison but not Amy.

I noticed Madison, in particular, when I sensed someone

standing close behind me even though the police officers had cleared the immediate area of everyone except emergency personnel and me and Marge. Had they not shooed Madison away because she was Madison Twombly? Had she tucked herself so close to Marge and me that they simply assumed she'd been with us in my Bug? Whatever the reason, Marge explained her issue with her pneumonia and was allowed to be questioned in the warmth of the squad car, but Madison stayed with me.

There had been no problem in tracking Lilly's path to the road. Her studio, because of all the combustible gases and such used to do her welding, was not only on the ground floor of the Yerkes arts building but it also had an exterior emergency fire door of its own. Her trail went from that door across the snow-covered lawn, not the shoveled sidewalk, to the edge of the eastbound side of North Star Drive and over the median to where she had landed in the westbound lane.

I told the officers that Lilly said she'd been accosted, and had given us the impression that the man had followed her.

"If the man followed her out of the building," I explained, "he only did so for as far as he had cover between the music and art buildings because Marge and I never spotted him. We only saw Lilly."

The two officers dismissed me, and Madison too, although they'd never asked her a thing, and went off to check Lilly's trail through the snow.

My crochet class students were huddled together against the crime scene tape barrier that the officers had strung up between the trees along the street. At the time they strung it, they hadn't talked to anyone so they couldn't have known Lilly had been running from an assailant. I guess it was the only thing they had had in their cruiser to cordon the area off from gawkers.

"Well, everyone," I said as I walked up to my students. "They've finished with Marge and me so I want you all to head over to Cornelia House for class. Marge and I will be there in a few moments. We need to get the Bug out of here and parked at the house."

With a smattering of affirmative replies, they turned to make their way through the crowd. I turned, expecting to see Madison right behind me, but she wasn't. She had stayed by the ambulance. For some reason she was right in the middle of everything, near the open rear end of the ambulance. She turned my way as the paramedics shut the doors, ready to head to the hospital.

"Emory!" She waved me over. "I'm going to go over to the hospital, change into my scrubs, and see what I can find out about all this." She paused before giving me a sly grin. "You'll just have to come up with a good excuse to the rest of the class since I told them earlier that I was really looking forward to class time today. Which I was, but …"

Madison paused. She suddenly looked very much like her father.

"I have this feeling I should go to the hospital." The grin faded. "Make sure my Mama knows where I am. I don't want her worrying about me on top of everything else. Ah … tell her I went to the hospital so I could give a more personal report to Papa about how Ms. Comfort is doing. She'll understand that, I think."

"Okay. I'll take care of it all at my end." I nodded briskly. "You just watch yourself, young lady, all right?"

"Yes, Ma'am!"

With a perky salute, she headed off eastward toward the hospital at a fast jog.

Chapter 14

THE CLASS TIME WENT WELL, CONSIDERING THAT MOST EVERY-
one wanted to focus more on the incident with Lilly than on yarn
and crochet projects. They wanted to know what Marge and I had
found out, if anything, from talking to the police, EMTs, and paramedics, and what theories we might have. Iga had come over to
the guesthouse with the Twomblys, as Henri had. I had sent Iga
up to tell Amy where Madison was when she met us at the door.
Since then, she had been hovering around the edges of the room,
listening in on everything. Henri kept popping out of the serving
entrance at the far end of the room from where we all sat, gathered
near one of the large room's two fireplaces. He had laid out hot
and cold soft drinks of various kinds and an array of munchies

and finger foods on a long table there, and he kept rearranging and replacing items as an excuse to be in the room. Not that we weren't taking enthusiastic advantage of the buffet, but I'm sure things weren't being consumed that quickly.

The first floor of Cornelia House was set up for entertaining only. There was the room we were in, intended for cocktail parties and receptions, which ran the entire depth of the house on its western side. The Mission-style furniture in the room was sparse for such a large room, but that was to make it easier to set it up for gatherings where people are expected to mostly be standing and walking around mingling. The sofas and a few easy chairs were grouped by the fireplaces and were the original aged oak, but the cushions were newer and covered with either chocolate brown or beige leather. When events were being hosted in the room, classic wood folding chairs with padded leather seats would be added along the walls. The coffee tables in the two groupings doubled as benches and, with the addition of pads, joined the folding chairs along the walls during parties. On the eastern side of the house was the dining room, with its oak Mission-style table that could seat twenty-four people, and the large kitchen, part of which extended off the back of the house into the back yard. A butler's pantry with a wide hallway ran from the kitchen to the parlor to facilitate the serving of light party fare if an occasion didn't include a full meal, or punch and hors d'oeuvres before a meal. Two restrooms were situated on either side of the stairs to the upper level, at the rear of the entrance hall. All guest living quarters were on the second floor and the house's design included a small elevator at the back of the parlor, one of those lovely old grillwork cage styles large enough for a wheelchair and an assistant, should any guests require the use of one.

"We really don't have much to tell you all," I said to the group after the same questions came up for the third time. "Really. Professor Comfort passed out there in the street without saying a thing to us."

Marge and I had quickly discussed what and what not to tell as we drove the Bug over to the house. We'd decided the less said about an assailant, a red bow on a delivered coffee cup, and a drugged teacher—well—the less said the better until we knew more about how the authorities were going to handle it.

"I think Madison might have headed over to the hospital," Marge chipped in. "Most of you know she volunteers there and I think she's hoping that some of the nurses might tell her something. We'll all know more later." She looked around at everyone. They had all been working on their crocheting as they bombarded us with questions. "Does anyone have a spare crochet hook? I'm tired of just sitting here with nothing to do with my hands."

"I've got one." Tom waved his left hand while digging into his duffel bag with his right. "Need any yarn?" he asked as he produced the hook.

"No. Only my skein of white got ruined as it was the color I was currently working with. I have the other two colors I can fiddle with." Marge held her skein of yellow aloft, exhibiting it as if it was a sports trophy she'd just won.

Marge had walked in, still carrying her unfinished afghan that I had used under Lilly's head. It and the attached skein of white yarn had gotten soaked through with muddy slush and a bit of blood from a scrape on the side of Lilly's face. Iga had promptly confiscated it all, promising she could wash the part Marge had crocheted. She had tied off the yarn and cut it free, first, since she said she couldn't wash it without it becoming a tangled mess.

Marge said that was fine and it all was whisked off to the laundry room in the basement.

"Emory, can you show me how to make a granny square?" Marge asked as she took the hook from Tom.

With that the class settled into its usual pattern of everyday chatter and good-natured joking around.

"Emory! I need to speak with you."

Amy Twombly's voice cut through the cheery exchanges in the foyer of Cornelia House as we all said goodbye to each other and to Iga and Henri.

All eyes looked up to the railing across the large landing that fronted the second floor of the house.

"Now," she ordered as though I was one of her household staff.

I resisted the urge to curtsey and bow my head. "I need to take Marge home, Amy, but I can …"

"No. Now. I need to speak with you, *now*. Isn't there someone else who can … Didn't any of the others drive here?"

Naomi touched my shoulder. "I've got this, Emory," she said softly. "No problem. I'll also let Jebbin know you're staying here a bit longer."

"Okay," I called up to Amy. "I'll be there in a sec, just let me see my students out first."

She huffed, turned on her heel, and marched toward the back of the house. I knew there was a nice lounge area that opened up off the landing.

"Thanks, Naomi. You'll need Jebbin's cell number." I started to dig in my purse, berating myself for never having memorized it—cell phones and contact lists make it too easy.

"Nope," she assured me. "I'll just call the college switchboard and they can put me through on the lab's phone."

"Yes. Yes, that'll work. Thanks again, Hon. Ah ... bye, everyone, and I'll see you tomorrow."

The class headed for the door to freedom. With a sigh, I headed for the stairs of doom.

Upstairs, Amy sat on the edge of a beautiful damask Queen Ann chaise. Her pale, elegant hands lay clenched and white-knuckled in her lap.

"Sit down." She didn't look at me, only jerked her head to indicate the matching settee across from the chaise and I set my craft bag and myself down. "What was all that about?" The bitchy tone was back in her voice, and her eyes, looking past me, not at me, were cold.

"What was all ..."

"The class." She cut me off quick and heavy, like a meat cleaver. "The class. All the students. Henri making food and Iga doing laundry for some strange reason. I heard the machines running. And ..." Amy shivered. "And *crocheting*. After everything. After ... after ..." Her voice trailed away and for a moment she stared at nothing, her eyes empty, before a strange look filled them. "And Madison."

The last syllable hissed as she finally looked at me. The hiss had been that of a steam kettle. Rage now simmered in her big blue eyes.

"Madison?" Minnie Mouse had borrowed my vocal chords.

"She was up here, with me like she has been since ... She was up here and there were sirens, close by, and she excused herself and ran down the stairs and out the front door. Then, after a very long time, while I'm getting more scared by the minute, Iga comes up to tell me there'd been some sort of accident that apparently involved someone from the college and that you … *you* … sent her up to let me know that my Maddy had run off to the hospital to check on the stupid college staff person. And when I asked why you were the one who had sent her up, Iga told me it was because Maddy had asked you to, since you were going to be downstairs with the *crocheting* class."

In one sharply graceful move Amy was up and pacing with a vengeance. For whatever reason, it was then I noticed that she was, as usual, meticulously dressed and coiffed, though her flowing silk pants seemed a bit long. As soon as I thought it, I knew why: even when she had been seated, I hadn't been able to see the tracking bracelet around her ankle.

She pulled to a halt in front of me.

"I would have gone down there and let you have it right then, but I was so upset I was afraid I'd … How *could* you? Whatever in that puny little homemaker's, crafty person's mind of yours made you presume to bring the … the *crocheting* class here? Made you take over my household. Commandeer my house keeper and chef!"

"It was Madison's idea." Minnie had let go of my voice—now I sounded like I had laryngitis.

"It was …"

I cut off the crescendo she was building to.

"Madison's idea, Amy, not mine." My low, raspy voice continued, but her homemaker comment had me riled. I stood up. "Jairus called on Monday, during class, because he wanted to personally let the class know why you and Madison weren't there. Not that he really needed to, because I don't think there was a person alive in Twombly who didn't know where you were. I think he just felt a need to talk to people who … well, he thought the people in the class had become your friends to at least a small degree. Yours and Madison's. I think he wanted to talk to people he hoped cared about you and your family."

Amy had started to shrink before my eyes from the moment I told her that Jairus had called. Well, not really, but she'd gone from a commanding, space-dominating presence to a shaken woman who walked unsteadily back to the chaise and sat down.

"Madison came into the room, at his end of the call, realized he was talking to us and asked if she could talk. When she came on—the phones were on speaker, so everyone could hear—she asked if I would be willing to have the class meet here. She said she wanted to see us and still be in the class. She offered Henri's services to provide our lunch as well."

I walked over and went down on one knee so that I wasn't looming over her. My boney knee dug into the floor but I focused on Amy.

"She said she wasn't sure you'd want to join us, but I could tell by her voice that she was hoping that if we met here you might eventually come down. She really wants to stay with you, you know."

"Then why'd she …" Tears had started to drip from Amy's eyes and she paused to sniff, but her accusatory tone persisted. "Why'd she run off to the stupid hospital, if that's really where she went? I mean, I might not be needing an ambulance or a hospital, not yet at least, but I need her here."

I hesitated.

I wanted to tell Amy why I thought her daughter had taken off after Lilly, but I wasn't sure she was in any mood to process the information. Yet …

"I'm going to be straight with you, Amy. I just, ah … feel it's the right thing to do. Am I reading you right? Do you want the real reason?"

I was surprised. Amy sat up straighter, waved for me to grab a tissue from a nearby box for her, and nodded to me as I handed it to her.

"Okay, here goes. You were an acting major in college. All right, you are now playing a fourteen-year-old whose family has been bulldozed with sudden disaster. You're bright. Curious. You're hurting worse than you ever have in your life. You with me?"

Another nod.

"An opportunity arises to be distracted for a while. Not only distracted but you can feel useful, ah … like you can really help in some way, which you can't do with the mess at home. What happened to this other person might have something to do with another bad thing that's been going on where your character lives. Something that hurt a girl she knows. Now, how would you play that character? If they let you ad-lib, what would you do?"

Amy sat quietly. I could almost hear her thoughts as they made their way around in her mind.

"I feel so bad," said a young girl's voice. Not like Madison's. Not even that much like Amy's. It was the new character's voice. "I can't get involved with Mom's … case. No. They'll be watching me and won't like it. I'm her kid. But this other person, just 'cause they work for Daddy's college … well … That's not the same."

Her head came up from where it'd been planted in the tissue. Her eyes gleamed. She was grinning. Somehow she looked even younger than her teenaged daughter. She actually must have been a pretty good actor, I thought. Only a wee bit grudgingly. And, as I had hoped, her mind had blended real life with her impromptu performance.

I was seeing a talented actress actually becoming someone else.

"I already volunteer at the hospital." She got up, walked to the window and looked out. She hadn't looked at me. I wasn't there. "If I go to where the sirens are heading, nobody will notice or care if I hang around and, you know, listen. Then, I can go to the hospital and be in the ER or the victim's room, move things out of the doctor and nurse's way. Hang up the person's clothes or something. You know, just be the invisible teenaged volunteer. And ..."

Amy paused then turned to face me. Looked me square in the eyes. She knew.

"And I could do what I can't do for Mama and Papa," Amy's own voice was strong; the earlier bitchy, defensive tone was gone. "And for a little while I can catch my breath and be myself again." Another pause. "That's it, isn't it?"

"Yes," I replied. "I think Madison saw a chance to have some space, to deal with someone else's problem for a while. Well, it still is Jairus' problem, in a way, since it involves the school, but the college is the college. It's not her family. You are her Mama and Jairus is her Papa and that's a whole different thing."

"That's why ... why Maddy wanted the class here, too, isn't it?"

I had to think about that one. "Hmm ... I think so, yes. At least partly. I really do think she's hoping you'll come back and be with us. You know, people in the class know you at least a little and consider you part of their group. I think she's hoping that, even though it's crocheting, you'll come down, be with the group, and forget for a while ... well, maybe not forget, she's smart enough to know that won't happen, but at least be distracted for a while."

"Yes." Amy nodded as she turned away from the window. "She's more than smart enough. I think I'd better let you go now. I'm ... I'm sorry you've had to live through another of my bitchy moments."

I was still down on one knee and it was probably a good thing, as I might have lost my balance from the shock had I been stand-ing. Amy Twombly had just admitted to having "bitchy moments"! Amy Twombly had just *apologized* for having bitchy moments. Heck! The only times I had seen Amy *not* be bitchy was when she had to be the model rich-man's wife around Jairus or people she knew were important. I had to make a concerted effort not to let my surprise show on my face as she offered her hand to help me up.

"Apology accepted, though not needed." I got to my feet, gath-ered my crocheting things, and preceded her down the stairs. She called Iga to fetch my coat and hat, then watched me bundle up. "I can't imagine what you're going through," I said as I settled my hat on my head. "I'm amazed you're holding up as well as you are."

Amy walked me to the door.

"Thank you." She sounded weary. "It's mostly because of Jairus and Maddy, well, Iga and Henri too I suppose. Especially Iga. She is taking such good care of us all."

I opened the door and paused, turning to look at her as I smiled. "You're a marvelous actress, Amy."

"Thank you, I've had loads of practice," Amy replied as I stepped out onto the front porch. "All my world's a stage." She closed the door behind me.

I was in my Bug, doing up my seatbelt, before her change in the "All *the* world's …" quote filtered into my mind. Truly, we all play different parts as we move through life, but … her tone had been world-weary as she said it. A knowing tingle crawled up my spine and I realized there was a great deal I didn't know about Amy Suzanna Twombly.

Chapter 15

AS I DROVE HOME MY THOUGHTS TOOK A NEW TRACK. NOT ONLY was there a lot I didn't know about Amy, there wasn't a whole lot I knew about *anybody* who was involved with the case. After all, Amy had been in the house. Madison had been in the house—although she had been with me when the murder had actually happened. Iga had been there and so had Henri. Any of the adults in the Twombly mansion that day had had ample opportunity to kill Resie Schmid. I didn't know whether any of them had a motive to do that … and I didn't know anything about Resie either.

A quiver shivered its way up my back. The thought materialized in my head that I really needed to get some more lavender pillow spray from Aine McAllister at Mysterious Ways.

This intuitive nudge could have been better timed—I was already at the corner where I needed to turn. I yanked the steering wheel around, slid like a sidewinder across icy College Avenue and pirouetted onto Buttercup Street like a figure skater doing a sit spin. Thank the good Lord there weren't any cars parked on that stretch of Buttercup or I would have careened into them like a hockey player hitting the boards. I managed to straighten out and kept a grip on the pavement during the eleven blocks to Mysterious Ways.

"Hi, Emory!" Aine's cheery smile faded quickly as she grabbed my hand and walked me to a table. "Sit down, girl." She took the chair opposite me, her gaze never leaving my face. "You look haunted."

"Ah, no. No ghosts. Just … ah … took a spin around the corner at College and Buttercup." I made circles with my index finger to help her get the idea.

"Hmm. No. I can see the nerves from that, but they're on the surface. No. The haunted look is deeper. *And …*" She stressed the word, leaning in toward me across the small table, covering my still gloved left hand with her right. "And, I didn't say you saw a ghost. I said you look haunted."

I pulled my hand free of hers, took my hat and gloves off, and undid the top couple of buttons on my coat. Like most places that sell flowers and provide customers with samples of hot beverages, the shop was warm.

"Isn't that sort of what haunted means?" I flippantly tossed the words at her. "Ghosties and ghoulies and things that go bump in the night?"

"'She was haunted by the memory of her lost love.' 'He was haunted by the smell of hay, like on the farm where he grew up.'

"The strange old song haunted her dreams.'" Aine sat back with a smile as mysterious as her shop. "Not all ghosts are the spirits of the dead."

Warmth, as though I'd had a cup of Aine's calming tea, eased its way from my chest outward and I knew why I'd been sent to the shop.

"Yes. You're right. All sorts of ghosts can haunt folks. There are ... all sorts of ghosts."

"Hmm-mm," she agreed as she rose. "Lavender pillow spray?" She was already moving to the shelf where the sprays were displayed.

"H-how'd you know that?"

"How'd you know you had to come here?" She looked profoundly wise ... until she laughed. "I know you well, my dear, and customers love to talk to shopkeepers. Talk is that you and Madison Twombly have met for lunch. Witnesses say you and Madison Twombly were both at the scene when you almost hit Lilly Comfort. There's been a kidnapping, an attempted kidnapping, a murder, and Jebbin runs the forensics lab. I'm figuring that you need some help sleeping."

I relaxed a little. "No special magic?"

She put the pillow spray into a "Mysterious Ways are the Best Ways" bag, walked over to the teas section, and tucked a few more items into it before setting it all down by the register.

"Oh, I didn't say that, though most of my magic is more Holmesian than thaumaturgy. I know. I observe."

"And I noticed you said 'most' of your magic." I headed up to the counter as I opened my purse. "That leaves you some squiggle room for things of a more paranormal nature."

"Does it?" Her eyes sparkled like moonlight on the ocean waters that their color resembled. "That'll be fifteen fifty-six, Emory."

I handed her my debit card then picked up my bag of goodies when the transaction was completed. She walked back to the table with me, watching as I buttoned up my coat and donned my hat and gloves. Neither of us had said another word.

"Night, Aine, and thanks for … everything."

"Hmm, yes. You're most welcome and drive carefully, heading home."

The door had almost closed behind me when I heard her say, "I always leave some squiggle room."

It was three-fifteen by the time I got home. I needed to call Jebbin about dinner.

"Hi, Hon." His soft Ozark accent drawled a tad slower than usual.

"Hi, Sweetie. Have ya had a busy day? You sound tired."

"Not busy," he paused. "Not that busy at all."

I understood the message beneath the words. "What we talked about Monday night?"

"Most likely but, I'm hesitant to just say yeah. Some things did come in to do for Lilly's case." I could hear his grin growing in his voice. "Fancy you being there, Miss Marple-Crawford. You and Nancy Drew-Twombly, from what I gather."

"I, at least, could hardly help it as Lilly landed right in front of Marge and me in the Beetle. Nancy Drew showed up of her own accord. Nothing of my doing. All that aside," I steered us back to his work, "what came in from the hospital?"

"As usual, we're doubling up on Antonia's fluids work. It'll help that we have a suspect—the Flunitrazepam. We'll be keeping an eye out for that now, as well as other date-rape drugs. And we have her coffee cup with the ribbon. The guy apparently was so intent on either chasing her or getting outta there after she got away that he didn't pick it up from where she dropped it before she ran."

I looked at the clock on the wall in the kitchen.

"I hate to cut you off, Hon, but I need to know about dinner for you two. You and Chatty can fill me in on the rest when you get here … if you can make it home, that is."

"Yeah, it shouldn't be any problem. Just a sec, Emory."

I heard some indistinct talking and then Jebbin came back on.

"I'm back, Sweetie. The crochet hook from the murder has finally made its appearance here. Chatty and I are going to process it, start all the computer searches, and then we'll be home for a quick dinner."

"Gotcha. You'll be wanting to hurry back to wait for results at the lab."

"Yep. That's my knowledgeable wife. See you about … ah, it's twenty to four … um … Make it five-thirty or six-ish."

"Will do, see you guys then."

I looked in my freezer freezer, as opposed to the fridge freezer, to see what I had on hand that would be yummy, filling, and quick to eat. Although with Jebbin, most anything rated as quick to eat. His mother often told me, "I've no idea 't all where the boy got that habit from. Rest of us like to taste our food."

Doing another Impossible Pie would fit the bill, but I didn't want them wearing out their welcome.

Ah ha!

I pulled a package of stew beef out of the freezer, a couple containers of frozen beef stock from pot roasts past, and a bag of frozen stew vegetables. Just add some instant mashed potatoes to thicken it, close to serving time, and I'd have a hot, hearty meal for my hardworking forensic scientists. I checked the fridge. Yep. I even had a can of crescent rolls that I could bake, along with some corn muffins I could make up from a mix, so the guys and I would have nice hot, fresh bread for soppin' up the thickened broth.

The kitchen was smelling all yummy from the simmering stew just as I heard the little tune my phone plays when I have a new text message.

It was from Madison.

M. - *Home now. Have some info. Want to chat later tonight. Are you on Skype?*

I tapped my phone. *Yes. Use it with Molly & Lanthan. bg.fiddler12*

M. - *maddyhatter.317, 10 tonight too late?*

E. - *Nope, see ya then.*

M. - *K*

I wondered what the girl had found out, and how she'd found it out, then I laughed out loud. Kumquat was rubbing my ankles and looked up at the sound. "Mama's laughing at Miss Madison's Skype name," I informed my fluffy orange cat as I stroked her cheeks. "'Maddyhatter'. It fits her I think. Wouldn't surprise me at all to have a wacky tea party with that girl and enjoy every minute of it."

Kumquat gave me one of her silent meows while, from across the kitchen, Hortense "meow-ooo-ed". From her bed in the corner, Sophie stirred, rose, and clickety-clicked across the linoleum to sit down in front of me and stare into my eyes.

"I know, I know, guys. Outside time for the big doggy and food time for one and all."

They all smiled at me.

The "kids" were fed, the stew piping hot, the breads were ready to come out of the oven as Jebbin and Chatty came through the front door. To say this was a hurried meal was putting it mildly.

Although the fellas didn't just start grabbing, like Jebbin had once done, still they hardly paused in their shoveling long enough to give me any news before they were done. I didn't know Chatty could eat that fast. The man usually savored every mouthful of whatever I fed him.

"D'lushious!" he muttered around a mouthful of stew and corn muffin.

"Hm-mmm!" Jebbin grunted affirmatively, nodding.

"Got finger prints off the coffee cup." Jebbin took a few seconds to speak with an empty mouth so I could understand him.

"So far no hits anywhere, but we have not yet received the prints the city police took from workers at the coffee shop and Dr. Comfort." Chatty filled in.

"Some kind of oil on the crochet hook, we think." Jebbin got that out while soppin' up with a crescent roll.

"Running sample through gas chromatograph." Chatty spooned up a broth-soaked chunk of corn muffin.

"Prints on hook. Most likely Amy's. We'll run 'em when we get back." Jebbin stood up and headed for the sink with his empty bowl.

"They are not as good as we hoped. They're at least partially smudged. We will figure that out soon." Chatty followed Jebbin to the sink.

A kiss on the cheek from Jebbin. A huge smile from Chatty. Thanks and goodbyes from both, then they threw on their coats and were gone.

Chapter 16

I SAT AT THE DINING TABLE FEELING AS IF I'D JUST DONE TEN minutes on my exercise bike. If I'd had time to eat more than a couple of spoonfuls of my stew I'd be surprised. I got up, found my Kindle, put it on its stand, and settled in to read and eat at a much more congenial pace. Hortense and Kumquat did their floating cat jumps onto opposite ends of the table, where Jebbin and Chatty had sat moments before, curled up on the placemats, and took cat-naps. Sophie went under the table to be a furry footrest for her mom.

When I finished eating I cleared my dishes, started the dishwasher, made up a mug of the "Cogitation Tea" Aine had put in my bag—I'd often told her I needed all the help I could get to keep my thoughts straight—grabbed my laptop, made up a fire in the fire-place, and then plopped myself into my chaise to do some thinking while I waited for the Skype call with Madison.

I opened Skype, so I wouldn't get distracted and forget later, then opened a blank word processor document. "Who Killed Resie Schmid?" it proclaimed top and center on the page.

"Good question," I said to Hortense who was curled up by my feet.

"Rwow," she agreed.

I typed my list of suspects down the left side of the page.

Amy Twombly

Madison Twombly

Me

Henri the chef

Iga the housekeeper

Oh yes. I was really making progress here.

"Well, Miss Hortense Kitty, Mommy can cross herself off because I *know* I didn't do it. A-n-d … I can put a line through Madison—a.k.a. Nancy Drew—Twombly because we were together in the family room when we heard Amy arguing with Resie in the dining room and we were both in the family room with Amy until she went back into the dining room."

My mind sing-songed; *Amy Twombly, with the crochet hook, in the dining room.* I shook the thought away. This wasn't a game and I hadn't a clue.

I wondered if Aine's tea to aid my thinking was doing me any good.

I put a strikethrough line across my name and Madison's.

"That leaves Amy, Iga, and Henri. But I already had figured that much out so it isn't much help to have done this."

Hortense blinked at me. "Mer-ow-ooo," she intoned, sounding rather disappointed with me.

I made a page break and centered Amy's name at the top of the page, then sat and stared at it. I hated that I kept starting with her because I really, really, really didn't think she'd done it. Really. She just always came to mind first. Because she's a person you notice. Because she had all the motive and opportunity in the world. Because I could picture her doing it in a fit of rage. Because …

There seemed to be a whole world of "becauses" and I didn't believe a single one of them.

So …

I looked at my mostly black tuxedo cat.

"Help me out, here, Hortense."

She opened her eyes a little wider.

"Amy Twombly. Do you think she did it?"

Not even the tiniest twitch of a whisker.

"Iga the housekeeper?"

No response.

"Henri the chef?"

Hortense yawned and laid her head on her front paws.

I tried asking Sophie. She didn't help any more than Hortense had, and Kumquat was a sweet girl but never much of a thinker, so I didn't bother asking her.

"On … my … own." I sighed.

I opened up my reminder, notes, to-do-list program and typed in: *Ask AnnaMay*. I smiled at the note. If I was a writer and wrote fantasy stories, she would be a wizardess. Yes, wizardess, as in a female wizard. Not a sorceress. Not a witch. Wizards often have a nicer reputation than sorcerers and sorceresses, or witches and warlocks. Gandalf was a wizard. Merlin was a wizard. The Wizard of Oz was a wizard. When I was a youngster, after I read *The Lord of the Rings*, I decided I was a wizardess. I liked the feel and sound of it.

AnnaMay is a wizardess!

The wizardess of research! The wizardess of the library!

I desperately needed to find out more about Iga and Henri. And Amy. And Resie.

My fingers resting on my keyboard went colder than usual.

"Not all ghosts are the spirits of the dead."

What was this phrase trying to tell me? It niggled at the back of my mind. It twitched the middle of my back. I'd gotten so busy with dinner. I'd gotten so busy with approaching this my usual way that I had forgotten what had happened at Aine's shop. I looked at the clock on my computer.

It was only seven-thirty. Madison wouldn't be "calling" me until ten. If I set my mind to working on this "message from wherever", I might be in the middle of some great insight just when she called and it would either interrupt my train of thought, possibly derailing it off a high bridge never to be recovered, or I might not be able to put my train on the siding while I talked to Madison and I wouldn't really hear a thing she'd say to me. Plus, she'd be seeing me. She'd see I was distracted and be hurt or offended by it and the dear girl didn't need that from me with everything else that was happening in her life. Or, the gentle rhythm of my thought train just might lull me to sleep and I wouldn't hear the alert for her call. I wished I had asked if she could call me earlier …

Skype alerted me to a call.

"You're early," I stated happily to a tired looking Madison. "I'm glad. I actually was just wishing I'd asked you to call earlier."

Her face brightened. "Cool! I'm a wish come true. I said ten 'cause I completely did not expect to be able to call until after my bedtime. But Mama said she was tired and went off to bed just a few minutes ago. Papa's in his study, so I thought I'd see if you were on yet."

"Worked out well," I replied. "Do you think your Mom's okay? She and I, ah, had a talk after crochet class. When, by the way, I found out you hadn't told her you'd invited us."

"Yeah. Ah. Bad move on my part. She and I talked when I got home from the hospital and she made it clear she thought that was a bad decision. The my-not-clearing-it-with-her part, that is. But, she seemed happy that you two had talked and she understood why I offered to have the class here, and," her eyes gleamed, "this is the best, she said she might even come down and join us. Maybe not tomorrow, but she's at least considering it. Isn't that awesome?"

"Awesome indeed. I've got a nice hook she can use. Doesn't look a thing like her Furls hook, so I hope that helps."

"Yeah, me too."

"Okay. To work now. What did you learn about Lilly's attempted abduction, Nancy Drew?"

Madison laughed. "I've read those books! Read the original ones and the newer ones. I liked the old ones better. I'll take being Nancy. She was cool and pretty daring for her times. How'd I end up being Nancy Drew?"

"Jebbin so dubbed you. Makes sense since I'm Miss Marple."

"We rock! I always thought she was one cool little old lady."

We both laughed. It felt so good.

"Okay. I'll tell you what I heard at the hospital if you tell me what happened before I got there. As I was running over to the accident, I saw you bent down by Ms. Comfort. Did she say anything?"

I gave Madison a summary of the conversation, which was

quite short when all of Lilly's pauses were left out.

Her enthusiastic expression faded as she listened. "I don't know that I have much more, then." She sighed. "She did wake up for little bits, here and there, and said a lot of the same stuff. About the bow on the coffee cup and about the guy's face being good to sculpt. Oh, and the blond hair not going with his dark eyebrows, she mentioned that, too. I figured either he dyes his hair blond, that's pretty common, or that he might have been wearing a wig as a disguise. Thing is, she might recognize him anyway since she was so fascinated with his facial structure. He didn't change his bones."

"Yeah. I thought about that too." I wasn't too much perkier than Madison now. "Drat! I was hoping she might have pulled up something new."

"Yeah. But, they figured she'd gotten the same drug as Tracy did, so her memories are apt to be hazy."

"Well. Jebbin and his forensic scientist colleague, Dr. Nibodh Chatterjee, have the coffee cup and the red bow, so we're hoping for an I.D. from some prints. Dr. Chatterjee, we call him Chatty 'cause he's so talkative, he's as good as Jebbin is. He owns an independent forensics lab and has helped Jebbin out in the past."

Madison looked down at her keyboard. "Sorry I wasn't more help."

"You did fine, Hon. In fact, there's something you can do better than I could."

Her head came up. Hope was in her eyes. "What?"

"I want you to think about Lilly's description of her attacker. Maybe dyed blond hair. Maybe darker hair. Dark brows and a sharp, clearly defined jaw, nose, and cheekbones. Start looking around yourself and asking amongst your friends from school …" I paused. Frowned, "Why are you in the crochet class? Isn't the

Twombly school district back in session?"

A blush colored her cheeks. "Yeah, but I'm a Twombly." She chuckled. "And even better, I'm nearly a straight-A student who has already been taking some college level classes, so I'm way ahead of where I need to be. Since Mama wanted to take the class, 'cause of Resie, and was wanting to spend more time with me, she pulled some strings so I could be in it with her. I'm taking the class for elective credit and I'm getting assignments and stuff from my regular classes that I work on in the evenings and over the weekends. Plus I have to turn in a report about the class and bring in my finished project so they know I actually crocheted something."

I nodded. "That makes sense. You're something else, young lady. So, as I was saying, see if you spot anyone around town or on campus who seems to look like the guy. Ask friends to look. We don't have the best description and I'm sure Detective Anderson will be doing that too. But, I sometimes think young people see more than us adults, especially when it comes to noticing each other. I have this feeling the guy's not old. You know. Probably college age."

"Sounds right to me, if he was delivering for Fill Your Cup. They hire mostly older high school kids and students from the college."

"*If* he was really delivering for the shop." I was shaking my head. "You know the police had to have gone there first, to ask who the deliveryman was. I bet we'll find out that our kidnapper made up some excuse to get the order away from the regular guy as he was on his way to Lilly's studio."

There was silence as we both looked at places other than our computer screens.

"Can you think of anything else we need to talk about, Madison?"

She looked at me and shook her head.

"Okay, Hon. See you in crochet class tomorrow?"

She smiled and nodded. "Yep. And maybe Mama, too. See you tomorrow, Emory."

"See you, too, Madison."

We both clicked off and I sat there wondering how trying to figure out two cases at the same time was going to work out. I didn't remember old Jane Marple or young Nancy Drew ever doing that, and I wondered, as I have before, What Would Jane Marple Do if this was one of her problems?

Chapter 17

"NOT ALL GHOSTS ..."

The words interrupted my concerns about working two cases.

"Not all ghosts are the spirits of the dead."

I turned off my computer. Moved it off my lap and got up to make up a fresh, hot, cup of tea. I dug into my Mysterious Ways bag, pulling out the pillow spray and setting it aside. There were three more of Aine's cute origami boxes of tea: "Sheep Counter's Tea", "Sleep Like a Log Tea", and "Divine Wisdom." I chuckled. I reckoned the "Divine Wisdom" was there in case the "Cogitation Tea" wasn't quite enough help.

Kumquat hopped up onto the kitchen counter, sniffed the three boxes, knocked "Sheep" and "Log" off onto the floor, then looked me in the eyes.

"Quat-kins!" I eyed her suspiciously. "Are you stealing Hortense's job? She's usually my intuitive kitty."

My orange fluff-ball patted my arm then head-butted my hand as I reached to rub her head.

"Well, I guess you have had your moments in the past, haven't you, girl? You want Mommy to make herself a cup of 'Divine Wisdom'?"

I got no response beyond her purr.

A few pinches of wisdom went into my tea infuser.

"Divine Wisdom", as it turns out, smells wonderful. Fruity. Spicy. Mellow. Perky. All at once, somehow.

My cup of wisdom and I went back into the living room where it steeped while I built the fire back up. I parked my rear and legs on my chaise, took the infuser out and set it on the small plate I used for that purpose, then leaned back into the smooshy cushion. For a while I merely inhaled the steam rising from my cup. I've never liked scalding hot tea or coffee.

After a bit, I took a sip.

It tasted even better than it smelled.

And I sat.

And I sipped.

And sipped.

And ...

... Mr. Johansen.

I didn't move for fear of disrupting whatever was happening and the memories flowed as smoothly as the sweet spicy tea.

It was in the church Dad pastored in Minnesota. Dear Mr. Johansen. He'd been at the church long before we moved there. Everyone loved him. He was a good husband and father, church member, and citizen. By the time we knew him he was a widower and his kids had all moved away. When he was diagnosed with a fast-growing cancer that was already too widespread for any treatment, the call went out to his kids and came in to my Dad.

Before his kids arrived from their faraway homes he was gone.

But he'd talked to his pastor—he'd talked to my Dad.

Years later, when Dad was no longer pastoring, he told me about that talk.

"Mr. Johansen wasn't really Mr. Johansen, Emory. He was Mr. Knutzen. He'd been a hard man. A tough talking, rough acting, heavy drinking man. He'd had a wife and a child," he'd explained.

And he had abandoned them for, as he'd told Dad, a "freer life".

"A year later, in the midst of one of those frigid upper Midwest winters, he heard on the news about the tragic deaths of a poor young woman and her child from the fumes of a faulty gas heater in the tiny, rundown trailer they were living in," Dad had continued. "His last name. Their first names. His wife. His child. And, Emory-girl, the blessing of guilt found him. It chased him from the big city where he'd gone to be 'free' and sent him to a small Minnesota town."

It caused him to change his name.

It caused him to change his ways.

No one there knew who he'd been.

And when he married her, even his new wife didn't know. Their children didn't know.

No one ever knew.

But Mr. Johansen never, ever forgot.

"Who I was. What I caused. It haunts my days and it haunts my nights, Pastor. To this day, to this moment, that other man and his cruelty haunts me," Mr. Johansen, or Knutzen, told my father as he lay dying in that hospital bed.

And Dad told me because, in a lesser way, it had come to haunt him too.

"Don't ever forget, Emory-girl. You can't run away from yourself 'cause you take yourself with you wherever you go."

And I remembered what Daddy had said, and what Mr. Johansen had told him.

And I knew what that message, which had been sent via Aine McAllister, meant for me.

Chapter 18

"ENOUGH BUTTERING ME UP, EMORY! ANY MORE AND I'LL BE SO greasy I'll slide off my chair."

I'd been giving AnnaMay my "You are a Wizardess!" treatment and, yes, laying it on rather thick. Poor dear. I hadn't even let her get in the building before I started. I'd been waiting for her outside the main door of Blythe Hall. Fortunately the temperature wasn't too cold this morning and the ever-present prairie wind had been a mere breeze.

It did help that I'd brought a thermos of AnnaMay's favorite high octane, full bodied, it'll-melt-your-spoon coffee from Fill Your Cup.

She took a big chug of it before continuing.

"You obviously want something, mere mortal. Speak and I'll see if your request is worthy."

"I need background information on some people and I know the school runs background checks on everyone they consider hiring. I just have this feeling that it's a service the Wizardess Queen of Research provides."

"Yes. Well. I do some of it. Most of it is jobbed out to a firm that runs checks as their actual business." My best friend paused. "Whom am I checking out? And don't tell me it's Amy Twombly."

"No." *Drat. I had thought about getting Amy checked, but since I knew she didn't do it, I could let that slide.* "No Twomblys involved. I want their housekeeper and chef checked out."

She pulled a pad and pen over and took the pen in hand. "Names?"

I restrained myself from jumping up and yelling woo-hoo. I also in that moment realized I hadn't come to this meeting very well prepared.

"I don't know. Well, I mean …"

AnnaMay gave me her Air Force supply sergeant look that she reserved for idiots.

"Ah … her first name is Iga, pronounced 'ee-gah', and the chef …"

"Is Henri. I've been to events and meetings at the Twomblys' just as you have." She tunked her pencil on the pad, bouncing it on its eraser. "Makes me feel elitist. I don't know their last names either."

We both sat in embarrassed silence for a few moments.

"You want this, Crawford, then get me their names and any other info you can manage without being rude or obvious. *And* be aware that Captain Henry and his deputies have already done all of this."

That left me wondering how much to say to my friend. Jebbin, Chatty, and I weren't sure how much the sheriff's department was checking into anyone but Amy, and we were having to handle those suspicions carefully.

"True, but I'm sort of looking for things they might not be looking for."

"Like?"

"Like ... um ... One of them changing their name at some point in time. Maybe not being completely honest about where they're from." I flipped my hand in an attempt to be casual. "You know. Stuff like that."

"Okay, but I still think Henry and crew will check for that sort of thing."

"Humor me?"

"Humph." She wrote a note to herself on the pad that I couldn't read. "And, if I have to use our background check company, who is paying for it?"

"Ah ... probably me. I'm guessing you're saying it wouldn't do well to have it billed to the college."

"No. Not really." She spoke as she wrote, *"Paid-for-by-my-overly-inquisitive-friend-with-delusions-of-Miss-Marple-hood."* Then she looked over at me. "You have homework. Get as much as you can while you're at crochet class. You're holding them over at Cornelia House now, correct?"

"How did you know that?"

"Wizard!" we said in unison.

"Yes, O mighty one." I rose and grabbed my coat and accouterments without making eye contact, as a proper minion should. "I will do my task and report back ASAP."

AnnaMay flicked her hand at me as I turned to go. "Begone. You only have fifteen minutes to get yourself and Marge Purtle over there on time to start class."

It helped that I'd stashed my crochet supplies in the back seat of the Beetle before I'd gone to pick up the coffee at Fill Your Cup. As it was, Marge and I were ten minutes late. Iga was cool and aloof when she answered the door. She had always been on the formal side, never getting too chummy even with faculty and their family members who'd been coming to the Twomblys' for years. But she was definitely becoming increasingly reticent. I checked myself. No, she was burdened. Weighed down. Only I wasn't getting any feelings one way or another if it was all for the family I knew she loved and cared for, or for herself.

Also, but this was a potentially good thing, Amy wasn't there. Madison let us all know that her mom was still considering rejoining the class but hadn't decided yet.

Which freed me up to send Madison off to fill in the blanks on the staff.

I got everyone going on their projects, then I pulled my small notepad out of my purse and made up a list of information I thought would be helpful to AnnaMay, added instructions for her at the bottom, then handed it over to Madison. She read it then got up to get herself some munchies from the breakfast buffet table Henri had prepared. She was almost to the table when I noticed the slight waggling of her index finger signaling me to follow her.

"I already know a lot of this," Madison softly told me as she put a sliced homemade English muffin into the toaster and pushed it down. "I know these guys, ya know. Iga *Lesko*," she stressed the last name, "has been our housekeeper since Grandma Twombly died and her housekeeper retired, which was between when Jam VII was born and when I was born. I've known her my whole life. And Henri *Boulanger*, although he hasn't been here as long, lives at our house just like Iga does, so his mail comes to our house and I've seen his full name on it."

I just love missing the obvious. I should have figured she would know about the people who lived and worked in her home.

"Okay. Duh on my part. I should've known you'd know. I guess just write out the stuff you know and then see if you can find out any of the rest before the end of the day."

Her muffin dinged and she pulled it out of the toaster with a pair of little tongs that had been put there, apparently, for just that purpose. She smiled as she spread the halves with peanut butter.

"Yep. I can do that. But, Emory?"

"Yes?"

"Won't dear, sweet Captain Henry have already done all of this?" She asked as she stuffed the notepad into the back pocket of her jeans.

I was getting tired of having that pointed out to me when a good reply slipped down from my brain and out of my mouth. "Yes, Madison, I'm sure he has, but I don't reckon he'll want to share the answers he got with us."

"Oh!" She looked up from the banana she was peeling. "Oh, good point! You're right. I don't think he shares well with others." She sliced the banana in half crosswise and lengthwise then put two quarters on each muffin-half. "That's all good then. I can tell Iga and Henri something along those lines if they wonder why I'm asking." Then, her brows drew together. "But why am *I* asking them instead of you? I thought you wanted me working on the Mysterious Red Kidnapper Case?"

I shrugged and grinned. "Cute name for it. I did and you will. But I think Henri and Iga will talk more easily to their dear little Madison than they will to some nosey lady they hardly know."

"You're right. They both love me," she chirped happily as she poured herself some milk. "See, Emory, you don't always miss the obvious." She grabbed her plate and hurried back to the group before I could respond to her dig.

After that Madison would excuse herself a couple of times each hour. She claimed it was to check on her mom, but I knew at least some of the times she was sleuthing.

I went home for a few minutes at lunch. Yesterday Marge's husband, Percy, had let Sophie out for me but he had an English department meeting over the class lunch break today. I used my time while waiting on Sophie to do her business to call Jebbin.

Since I was calling his cell phone, he answered with "Hi, Hon" instead of his more formal "Twombly College chemistry lab" greeting.

"Hi, Sweetie. I'm home for a few minutes to let Sophie out and thought I'd call. How's it going today?"

"Watchful."

"Watch … Oh! You're still being observed."

"Yep."

"Ah, well then. I'll save my Miss Marple fact-finding questions for dinner tonight. In fact, I was wondering if you might be able to invite Jason Anderson over. I'm curious about how they're doing with the kidnapping case."

"Can do. Breaks are allowed so I'll do it then."

"You're my sweet man."

"You're my sweet lady. Just a sec." I heard soft talking and then, "Chatty has requested another Impossible Pie of some sort. Hope that doesn't mess up any plans that were already in place."

I chuckled. "Nope, not at all. Any idea of what time you'll get home?"

"Unless something else pops up we should be breaking for dinner about five. That work for you?"

"Yes, it should. Don't forget to invite Jason."

"I won't. See you at five. Love ya."

"Love ya."

The crocheting class went along as it usually does—the rhythmic movements of hooks and yarn as background to discussions about life, the universe, and everything. What classes the college students were going to be taking when the full spring semester started, who was going out with whom and who had broken up with whom, dreams and hopes for the future, what TV shows and movies everyone was watching, and Marge and I throwing in occasional glimpses into the lives of settled, married couples whose kids were out on their own.

Henri was moving in and out of the kitchen more as our eleven o'clock lunch break neared. I could hear him muttering to himself—not the sort of muttering of a person ticking things off a list to make sure they have everything. I watched him. He had to keeping going back to fetch things as though he was distracted and couldn't focus on the task of setting out the meal. His movements were lethargic. Like Iga, he seemed burdened and as with her, I wondered whom he was burdened for?

Were they worried about themselves? The Twomblys?

Or was it guilt haunting one of them?

Amy joined us around noon and we all greeted her with smiles and hugs—even Tom and Ed—which seemed to flatter her.

I spoke to her as I dug about in my supplies bag. "I brought a hook for you, Amy, just in case you want to work on …"

I'd almost said "your afghan" but suddenly thought she might not want any mention made of the project she'd been working on before. The project she'd used as an excuse to invite me over that horrible Sunday afternoon.

"In case you want to work on something," I said instead.

"Ah, okay." She sounded hesitant. Unsure about the whole business of crocheting. Of handling another hook. Without even looking to see where she'd land, she sat down in a chair beside me where, until just moments before Amy had shown up, Madison had been sitting. Madison stood a few feet away protectively watching her fragile Mama. I think her Twombly giftedness had let her know that Amy would head over to me.

"Here it is!" I held the hook out to her with it lying across my palm so she could get a good look at it. "It's a standard metal crochet hook, size H, with a handcrafted handle added to it to make it more comfortable to use. Makes it look prettier too," I added, hoping that its lovely appearance would help her get over the fact it was a crochet hook.

Amy stared at the hook with its pearlescent white and grey handle for a long time. "It looks like it's made of marble." Awe tinged her voice.

"It does, but it's pearlescent white polymer modeling clay that's hand formed to have the grey swirled into it, then it's worked around the shaft of the hook, baked, hand sanded, and polished."

I smiled, but said nothing, as Amy slowly reached over and picked up the hook. She stared at it. I tried to read her face for signs of what she was feeling or thinking.

Nothing.

Blank.

Then she wrapped her fingers around the handle.

"I don't have any yarn," she whispered.

A lovely, pale minty green skein of yarn appeared by Amy's hand. "Use this."

Amy and I both looked up to see Tracy, reaching across Suzanne, offering the yarn.

"It's a really pretty color and this yarn is so cuddly soft. You should make a shawl for yourself, Mrs. Tw … Amy." Tracy paused to dig around in her tote and pull out a second skein of the mint-green yarn. "Here. One probably won't be enough to make a nice, good-sized shawl. You know." She laid both the skeins on Amy's lap. "A shawl that's big enough to really be warm and cozy, not just something that dresses up an outfit."

Amy was staring at the yarn in her lap and the hook in her hand. I saw the glint as a tear fell onto the yarn.

"Emory," she spoke more firmly than I'd expected her to. "Is there some other pattern you can teach me? Something easy but will make …" Amy looked at Tracy. The awkward, tight-lipped smile of someone who's crying graced her face. Oddly, she looked lovelier than I think I'd ever seen her look. She looked genuine. "Something that'll make a warm, cozy shawl."

"I don't have any patterns with me, but if Madison will let me use her laptop, I'm sure I can find just what you're looking for."

"I'll be right back with it, Emory," Madison said as she left the room.

I looked at Tracy. "Tracy, why don't you and Amy go check out the snack table while I look at patterns?"

"Sure!" Tracy took the yarn off Amy's lap and set it on the floor by the chair. "I'm thirsty anyway. You know, winter dry air and all," she chattered as she touched Amy's arm to encourage her to stand up. "There's apple-flavored sparkling mineral water. It's really good, Amy."

Amy stood, wrapping her arm around Tracy's. "I know. I'm the one who has Henri buy it."

They moved off to the buffet while I got busy on the laptop and the rest of the class got back to their crocheting. I found the perfect pattern on the site for the Prayer Shawl Ministry, had Madison print it off, and soon Amy was sitting between Tracy and Suzanne working on her new project amongst a group of friends.

Chapter 19

AS I WAS PACKING UP TO LEAVE, MADISON BUMPED INTO ME AND winked.

"Don't forget your craft bag, Emory," she said, though I wondered why until I glanced down and saw my small spiral-bound-notepad in the tote amongst the yarn and my crochet hook case.

"I won't. Thanks for reminding me, Madison."

I would look at it later, either while dinner was cooking and I wasn't needing to keep a constant eye on it, or after the guys had gone back to work.

Unless Jebbin didn't go back, which meant I wouldn't have time …

I'd have to work that out if the need arose.

Our furry kids were happy Mom was home. All three met me at the door: Sophie's tail wagging her hindquarters off, Hortense sitting and calmly staring at me, and Kumquat twining her way around my ankles, between my legs, and over my feet until she nearly tripped me. Soph was patted and let out, to her great relief. The cats both got their faces rubbed and chins scratched. Once Soph was let in and her feet wiped off, I fed them all their dinnertime wet food treats before starting work on dinner for the humans.

Tonight, per Chatty's request, I'd make another Impossible Pie. Actually, since there was hopefully going to be four of us, and Jason was a hearty eater, I'd make two Impossible Chicken Pot Pies.

I took out a frozen package of four Dolly Parton sized chicken breasts.

Yes. The package assured me that the chickens had not been given growth hormones.

But ...

I could swear the chicken breasts, all golden crispy deep-fried, I ate as a young'un weren't anywhere near this big. Which is strange, seeing as normally things we remember from childhood seem huge.

Hmm ...

Be that as it may, I took them out, put them in a covered casserole dish with some water, pepper, salt, and a bit of sage, then into the microwave to defrost and cook. While they were doing that I greased two ten inch pie plates and got out the rest of my ingredients—except for the frozen mixed veggies—and set it all out on the counter. Then, I got my little notepad out of my tote and sat at the kitchen table where I could have a cup of Earl Grey tea and keep an eye on the chicken in the microwave and the rest of the ingredients on the counter.

Hortense and Kumquat have no trouble jumping up onto the counters and anything near the edge is within Sophie's reach.

Madison's information was in tiny, neat printing.

> *Iga Lesko: Been with the Twombly family for sixteen years. Grandparents, along with their four children, fled Poland shortly before the Nazi invasion. Eventually arrived in the U.S.—Dearborn, MI. Iga & her siblings were born here—in Dearborn—so she never had an accent but she still can speak Polish. Grandpa worked at Ford Motor Co. Grandma & mother & eventually Iga all worked as housekeepers. Grandma had started a housekeeping company in Dearborn. Iga's brother took over the company when Grandma passed away—after that Iga traveled around U.S. living in different cities & working as a housekeeper. Ended up in Twombly, IL & eventually working for Twombly family.*

> *Henri Boulanger: Parents were from Quebec. He was born in US in Plattsburgh, NY, on the shore of Lake Champlain. Has forgotten most of the French he knew. Father was a short-order cook, Mom was a seamstress who worked out of their home. Henri wanted more than short-order cooking. Finished high school, worked his way into better quality restaurants as a waiter & then kitchen prep, saved his money for chef's school. It took several years. He went to Le Cordon Bleu in Ottawa, Canada. Worked in a couple five-star restaurants before hired as a private chef by the Thomlinson family of Cape Cod. Mom lured him away from the Thomlinsons.*

I was shocked when I saw another entry.

Amy Susannah (Morton) Twombly: Mama has never said a whole lot about her childhood or family. Papa says she's an orphaned only child. She had friends from college & some of her professors at their wedding & that was all. I know she played on a playground at her elementary school when she was a kid. Went to a day camp sort of program that was at the playground every summer where she liked doing the arts & crafts & reading contests. Never says name of school or where she lived exactly. She's from Chicago. She met Papa at Illinois State Univ. He was in grad school for MBA. She was an under-grad theater major. He liked working lighting for the plays—that's where they met.

After that Madison had written this: *Doesn't make Mama look too good, does it :-(*

And I had to admit—it didn't.

Jebbin, Chatty, and Jason arrived around five-fifteen, just as I was taking the second pie out of the oven.

"What is that most heavenly aroma?" Chatty called from the living room as the guys hung up their coats and took off their shoes in the entry area.

"That would be the most heavenly Impossible Chicken Pot Pies."

Chatty positively beamed. "Jebbin, my dearest friend, you remembered to ask for pie for dinner."

"I like them too," my dear man replied as they all took seats at the dining table.

"Impossible pie? Not sure I've ever heard of such a thing," Jason said as he looked toward the kitchen where I was carrying the first pie to the table.

"Emory will have to share the secrets with your wife, Jason. The ones we had the other night were most excellent."

I laughed as I headed back for the other pie. "I'm not sure I'd trust Chatty's opinion, Jason," I called from the kitchen. "He seems to love all my cookin'." I set the pie down before sitting myself down.

Since the pies are loaded with mixed vegetables, chicken, and the "bread" formed by the biscuit mix, a large salad bowl of mixed lettuces, Julianne sliced carrots, chickpeas, and shredded cheddar cheese was all that was needed to complete the meal.

For a few minutes we all ate in hunger-inspired silence.

"Well," Jason spoke up after taking a long drink of his iced tea. "I agree with Chatty, this is most heavenly chicken pot pie and, yeah, I'd like you to send the recipe to Diane. I think even Lydia will like this, and she's got to be just about the pickiest eater ever known."

"I'll scan it and email it over to her after dinner, Jason," I replied, all smiles, "and I'm glad you like it."

"And now," Jason began, but then stuffed another fork-full of pie and salad into his mouth. He calmly chewed and swallowed before continuing. "Sorry, that mouthful was talkin' to me. I'm figuring I was invited to dinner to talk business, meaning the kidnapping, the near kidnapping, and what we're doing and thinking about them both." He looked at each of us, his eyes sparkling and his smile, always bright against his chocolate brown skin, widened as he did. "Yep. I'm right. What'cha want to know?"

As if I didn't already feel like a cat by an open birdcage, Jebbin and Chatty both turned to stare at me too.

"Well, you are the one who insisted I invite Jason, Hon. Don't keep the man waiting," Jebbin teased.

I looked them all squarely in the eye as I set my fork down. "All right. Guilty as charged. And speaking of charges, is there a suspect yet, Detective Anderson?"

Chatty and Jebbin dug back into their dinner, but kept glancing up at Jason and me to let us know they were listening in.

"At this time, sorry to say, no. As I'm sure our two forensic scientists already know, there were prints on the coffee cup. We took prints off everyone who worked at Fill Your Cup that day, the usual delivery kid's, and Dr. Comfort. All the prints on the cup were accounted for that way. The only thing the perp alone would have handled was the bow, and there were no fingerprints on the ribbon the bow was tied with. Our perp must have good dexterity and tied the bow with gloves on. Kinda a side note here; the fact that it's winter isn't helping us in the finger print department. The fact that it's cold out and most everyone is wearing gloves makes it easy for all sorts of petty criminals to cover up their fingerprints. They don't look suspicious wearin' gloves like they would in warm weather."

"You really think you'd be able to match the kidnapper's prints?" I asked. "From what I've heard, the theory is the kidnapper is young, maybe upper high school or college age."

"That can make it less likely, unless the kid's got priors. But still, it's worth a go as a lot of schools and police departments offer fingerprinting of elementary school students. You know, missing child concerns and such. So, actually, there is a fairly good print base for young people even if they haven't been in trouble. But, all those programs are voluntary, so we don't have everyone."

I nodded. Sorry to say, Jason was the only one not getting

much of a chance to eat.

Jebbin must have noticed it too.

"Good place for me to jump in with some info on the murder case since it has to do with fingerprints. You go ahead and do some eating, Jason."

Jason grinned and dug in.

"We got an I.D. on the prints on the fancy crochet hook," Jebbin began. "Those partials are Amy's. No doubt about it. That said, it is her hook and she had been using it to crochet, so you'd expect her prints on it."

"The oil we found on it," Chatty put in, "is olive oil. A coating that was thick in some places and thinner in others, like might be left by someone with the oil on their hands grabbing and holding the hook. And the thicker areas were only on the handle part of the tool—not where the hooked part is. Our readings indicated the entire implement had olive oil on it but the hook end was mixed with the aqueous humor and vitreous humor from the eye."

I could have forgone the last bit, but I was used to such table talk at this point in my life.

"The oil on the body of the hook had traces of spices in it. Sage, rosemary, and garlic, which made us wonder if Henri might actually be the murderer." Jebbin's turn again. "But it isn't a definite as the family had what Henri described as 'spaghetti with a light tomato sauce' for Sunday lunch along with Italian bread with seasoned olive oil for dipping. So Amy could have had residue from the dipping oil on her hands. Still, with the thickness of the oil layer in some places, Henri can't be discounted."

"What we can't quite figure is what olive oil was doing on the hook anyway, especially on the actual hook part of it."

"Oh! I just remembered something." I hated to bring it up but felt I'd better. "You're supposed to clean the hook with olive oil. Amy told me about it the first day of crochet class. I'd never seen a hook like it, so I asked her about it after class. She'd already put it away in its box, but she took it out to show me. A small card with information about her specific hook and care instructions had fallen on the floor. When I picked it up to return to her, she showed it to me and said that she'd already oiled it a couple of times, even though the directions said once a month."

Jebbin nodded in acquiescence. "That explains that. Shame it leaves Amy in the picture."

"Yes, we were hoping we had something to turn the sheriff's attention elsewhere." Chatty said after swallowing some of his lemon mineral water. "We told our watcher, who was a good boy and told Captain Schneider, who came to talk to us about it. Of course, we have no idea what he'll choose to do with the information."

The last part of Chatty's comment hung in the air like a whiff of litter box.

Jason cleared his throat. "Well, fingerprint evidence, or lack of it, hasn't made much difference in the kidnap case." He continued with what he had been saying before. "Everything's been pretty clean. As I'm sure Jebbin has told you, the red items that got left in dorm rooms were either totally clean, the girls had been creeped out and not touched them, or they only had the prints of the students they'd been given to on them. And it's the same with Lilly Comfort. Only prints on the coffee cup were, like I said before, hers, the workers at the coffee shop, and the usual delivery boy's."

"And, like you said, no suspects yet." I dished myself up a second piece of pie and some more salad.

It took a while for Jason to answer. He was busy eating.

"No." He took a drink, then continued. "Tracy never could tell us much. She thought he was wearing a mask of some sort. Nothing too weird or freaky, she didn't think, as she figured something like that would have been scary enough that she'd remember it. But she said the face just didn't look right to her. Then again, that could have been the Flunitrazepam. She did say he was a male, she could tell that much, that he was tall. A lot taller than her, she said, and thin. She thought his hair was red. Not carroty red, but red. Let me eat some more."

By now, Jebbin and Chatty were finished and Jebbin had taken two bowls out of the cupboard and was digging into the freezer to get the chocolate chip ice cream. I really did feel badly that Jason was the one having to do so much talking. He was certainly as busy with his part of the case as the two forensic chemists were with theirs, and I was sure that even if he went home after dinner, he wasn't finished for the evening any more than Jebbin and Chatty were.

"There gonna be enough of that for me to get some?" He looked at his half-full plate then over at the ice cream bucket.

"Oh, yeah," Jebbin replied with a grin. "I'll save you a scoop, Jason. Just you keep talkin'."

"A scoop?" Jason squeaked out, a sound not befitting his brawny build.

Jebbin laughed and held the open bucket up so we could see into the top. "There's plenty, Jason. It's three-quarters full. No worries."

"Better be, or I'm gonna take back all the info I'm giving out." He winked at me. "So, that's all we could get from Tracy—tall, skinny, red-haired—with a maybe on the hair color. Then, we have Ms. Comfort's description. The tall and thin is still there, but her kid was blond, though she did admit it could have been a wig because his brows were dark. So, he is making some attempts to conceal his identity. We're keeping our eyes peeled but don't figure we have much of a chance spotting anyone in particular. I mean, there's a lot of tall thin young men at the high school and at the college."

I suddenly remembered something Lilly had said to me about the boy saying weird things to her but had to be careful how I brought it up. I didn't want to tip my hand that she had talked to me and that Marge had overheard. "Did Lilly say anything about the kid talking to her? You know, anything weird like his 'You're not her' comment to Tracy?"

"Oh, yeah! Yeah, she did. Ah ... let me think. It was when they were still in her studio. She'd been drinking the coffee and he was still hanging around, which she said had already caught her attention as being strange—the delivery kids usually need to hurry back to the shop. Said something about he'd been looking for her. That he needed her help. Something along those lines. Oh, and this too. She said it was weird because he talked like she already knew him."

Chapter 20

BEFORE I COULD ASK ANYTHING MORE, A PHONE STARTED PLAY-
ing the theme from *Law & Order.*

"Mine," Jason said, leaning slightly to get it from his back pocket.

After a few grunted responses he said, "Yep, on my way," and
hung up. "Gotta go and I didn't even get any ice cream." He pouted,
looking a great deal like his youngest son, Justin.

I patted his hand as he pushed up from the table. "Next time
we'll have the ice cream first. Orange sherbet. We'll count it as a
fruit appetizer."

He laughed and gave me a quick hug around my shoulders.
"Sounds good, as long as it's not one of the times you invite Diane
and the kids along. The kids would start wantin' that all the time

and sayin' it must be okay 'cause Mrs. Crawford let them have ice cream first." He walked over to the closet after the hug and was putting his suit coat on. "I got what's left of an armed robbery at the Casey's out by the interstate to go check on."

"Anyone hurt?" Jebbin asked.

"No, but he did fire his weapon and damaged a couple of the coolers and stuff." He was stuffing his arms into his overcoat. "So I gotta go start the investigation. See you all later!" He waved as he closed the front door behind him.

In the meantime, Chatty had also stood up. "I will pass on dessert, this time, Jebbin. Use the bowl you got for me to serve some to Emory. As we discussed earlier, I will go back to the lab and see if everything is doing what it should be and then retire to my hotel."

Like Jason before him, Chatty walked to the closet as he spoke and put on his coat and hat.

"Good night, dear friends, and thank you for again for a most wonderful meal, Emory."

"My pleasure, Chatty," I replied.

"See ya in the mornin', Chatty," Jebbin said as his friend and colleague went out the door.

"You're home tonight?" I got up and went over to where Jebbin was dishing up our ice cream.

"No. I'm going somewhere else tonight. Silly question, Mrs. Crawford. Of course I'm home tonight, if I'm not going to the lab."

I wrapped my arm around his. "Any plans, Mr. Crawford?"

"I thought a little banjo and fiddle jam session."

"Uh huh."

"Some cuddling on the couch while we watch an *Andy Griffith Show* episode on Netflix."

"Sounds nice."

He set the ice cream scoop down in the sink, then pulled me into a hug. "Then, I thought we might shoo the cats off our bed and move the cuddling into our bedroom."

I tiptoed to kiss his cheek. "Sounds even better."

And a wonderful evening was had by all ... except maybe for Hortense and Kumquat who got shooed off the bed.

I couldn't get back to sleep.

As nice as our evening had been, my dreams had been strange. Amy Twombly had been in a dank, smelly, olden-times-type prison cell. Captain Henry Schneider kept walking in, sporting a mustache like Snidely Whiplash from the old Dudley Do-Right cartoons, and harassing Amy. Meanwhile, our son Lanthan and his wife Felysse, and our daughter Molly and her boyfriend Freddy, kept trying to break Amy out of jail. Tracy Watkins and Lilly Comfort, wearing red choir robes, suddenly appeared and, like a Greek Chorus, started reiterating everything that had happened while a shadowy Ichabod Crane-like figure circled round and round them, trailing a wispy red mist as he went.

I knew where it had all come from. The two cases were obvious. Jebbin had mentioned talking to some other law enforcement people, and yeah, scuttlebutt had it that Captain Henry was walking a fine line between being cautious dealing with a high profile suspect and focusing obsessively on said suspect. And yes, a few had also heard rumors that Henry was going to get a reprimand if he didn't speed things up in the Twombly case. The kidnapping case had been the main topic of conversation at the dinner table.

Then, there was the fact that Jebbin and I had talked about our kids last evening while we had a wonderful bluegrass jam session. We both hoped we'd see Molly and Freddy this Friday since the roads were now good and there wasn't any more snow predicted. Lanthan's family were all doing well and very busy as always. We were hoping to go visit them over spring break.

But knowing the dream's inspiration hadn't dispelled the disquietude it had left in its wake.

It was 1:20 a.m.

I gave up and got up.

I considered making a cup of tea but didn't feel up to making any choices as to what kind to have. Although "Divine Wisdom" might be handy. I opted instead for that best of all warm comfort drinks—hot chocolate. I still had a selection to choose from. Lanthan's wife, Felysse, often got teas or hot chocolate mixes for me at Christmas time, but those choices didn't seem as consequential as Aine's mysterious teas. I chose a mix that had vanilla in it, mixed it, nuked it in the microwave then moseyed into the living room. I had set up a TV tray and my computer stand in front of the sofa and booted up the computer while I was making the hot cocoa.

I would distract myself by checking emails. Who knows? Maybe one of my friends on Facebook had posted a cute cat video or a good joke.

What caught my eye were emails from AnnaMay and Madison. Which to read first?

Whether I used first names or last, AnnaMay Langstock came before Madison Twombly alphabetically. I opened Anna-May's email.

Hi Emory (Plebeian Underling ;-)),

Here's what I've uncovered thus far:

Iga Lesko—everything on her checked out. No surprises. No motives for killing Theresie (aka Resie) Schmid.

Amy (Morton) Twombly—there are problems. Using all information on record (that I or my sources could access this quickly) she doesn't seem to have existed before she applied to and was accepted at Illinois State Univ. That said, she had to have had paperwork of various kinds to get into ISU—social security number and such. BUT although the Soc. Sec. number was (still is) legit, driver's license was valid, etc., it's like she sprang, rather like Athena from Zeus' head, fully formed from nowhere. There can be legitimate reasons for such a phenomenon, but they are few and far between. I hesitate to jump to the obvious conclusion, that she was running from some sort of criminal past, but I couldn't find anything about her prior to ISU. Obviously, she had tons of motive for wanting to get rid of Resie.

Henri Boulanger—one would almost think he and Amy were in cahoots—or at least knew each other in their non-existent pasts. Yep. He doesn't seem to be who he says he is either. We've got him applying to Le Cordon Bleu in Ottawa, Ontario, from a residence in upstate New York—at which time all his paperwork for application (including passport) were in good order. But if I try to go further back, things break down. The names he gives for his parents belong to real people, but they were both already in the U.S., in upstate New York, at the time he claims they moved here from Quebec. In fact, it seems they had the same last name but weren't married to each other and possibly not even related. So, like Amy, Henri may or may not have a motive for killing Resie.

We just don't know enough about his past.

I'm having my sources delve deeper into everyone except Iga. (You will be out a chunk of change, sorry to say.)

OH! I also checked out our victim. Theresie (Resie) Schmid is also a mystery. Records of her go back about as far as Amy's—Amy was 21 when she applied to ISU, Theresie shows up at a business school in Chicago at age 20. Henri applied to Le Cordon Bleu at age 24—but still, Resie seems to just pop up. No idea where she was before Chicago.

At this point, all I can say is that it is EXTREMELY weird that we have three people with nonexistent childhoods and early adult years in the same household. Personally, I would say there has to be a connection between two or all three of them and that connection will explain their mysterious pasts and the motive for Resie's murder.

I hope this all helps. As usual, now you have me insatiably curious about all of these people.

Love ya (as only a benevolent monarch can ;-)),
AnnaMay, Wizardess of the Library

I read the email through three times and it didn't help clear up the bewilderment I felt.

Curiouser and curiouser.

I replied, thanked AnnaMay for all the effort and good info, agreed that this did seem "extremely weird", and told her to give me the bill next time we saw each other.

Hoping that Madison would have something less enigmatic to say, I opened her email.

Hi Emory,
Well, I've not come up with too much on the Mysteri-

ous Red Kidnapper Case. The description simply isn't good enough. Although, my best friend Diane has a friend that I know but I'm not really friends with named Mary & Mary's older sister said there was a guy who she's had a couple of classes with at the college—art classes—who sorta, kinda, maybe fit the description. She said he's a good artist, does stuff in an older more realistic style than most of the students. She said he never seems very happy, not even when the profs praise his work. She said she had a class with him last semester and that he seemed a little paler and sadder than he had when she'd had a class with him the year before, but he'd never seemed scary-weird, just unhappy.

Beth, that's Mary's older sister who said all that, said she'd try to find out what his name is. She thinks he's named after some old, well known, mid 20th century painter whose name is like an old west gunslinger. But she didn't think it was exactly the same name. It's a shame she didn't know the guy's name or remember the artist's name. Or the gunslinger's name for that matter.

On the home front, everyone is just feeling worse and worse. Henri is grumpy. He's never grumpy. He's usually the stereotypical jolly fat person. A happy round chef like the ones they have on kitchen towels and placemats and stuff.

Iga is stiff. That's the only word I can come up with for her. Like if she relaxes she'll fall apart.

I'm missing their smiles and their hugs.

Mama is … not doing well. I think coming to class helped, while it lasted, but as soon as it was over she crawled into herself again.

Papa has been home a lot. I think he's worried about me.

I know he's scared about Mama. He and I spent this evening watching Sweet Home Alabama and eating all sorts of snack food. Not helping anything much, except we relaxed a little bit, even laughed a little bit.

I'm going to close now. I'll see you and everyone else at class in the morning. :-)

Oh—thanks for all you're doing for everyone—all you're doing for Mama, Papa, and me.

Hugs,

Madison

I sighed. What a horrible thing to have to go through. I copied and pasted AnnaMay's email into a Word document so I could remove the paragraph about Amy, changed the *"three people with nonexistent childhoods or early adult years"* to two people, then replied to Madison and said that I'd be praying for everyone in her family—and Henri and Iga too. Thanked her for passing along what she learned from Beth via Mary via Diane—told her I'd attached what a source of mine had found out, and asked her to let me know as soon as she heard anything more and I would do the same.

The furry kids were all asleep and I was feeling sleepy again myself. I shut down the computer and toddled off to bed, hoping that my dreams would be boring ones.

Chapter 21

I GOT UP AFTER JEBBIN WAS DONE IN THE BATHROOM—ABOUT five in the morning. He was sitting at the kitchen table gulping down his second cup of coffee from a chemistry mug our Molly bought him with "What did the cow say to Molybdenum and Oxygen?" on one side and "MoO" on the other.

"You're up early," I said through a yawn.

"At least I'm awake. But actually, didn't you hear my cell phone ring?"

"Obviously, I didn't. What's up?"

"I'm surprised you didn't hear it, you're usually the lighter sleeper. Anyway, it was Jairus." I knew the look in Jebbin's eyes when he turned to look at me. It never meant good news. "Of all the Henry Schneider things to do, the captain showed up at Cornelia House at four o'clock this morning to take Amy off electronic surveillance and into custody."

I stumbled to the nearest chair as I blurted out, "What! Why?"

"Yep, *what* is right. Apparently, according to Jairus, Henry got a call bright and early from Sheriff Watkins telling him he needed to move things along in the case. Henry chose to interpret that as a need to put her in jail." He chugged the rest of his coffee. "He also told Jairus that there's enough evidence to go to trial and the department wanted to keep the accused—and yeah, he called her 'the accused' instead of 'Amy' or 'Mrs. Twombly'—in a more secure situation."

Jebbin got up, rinsed his mug out, set it in the sink, and then headed for the front door. Sophie and I followed along.

"So, I'm off to the lab. I already called Chatty and he should be there soon." He pulled his stocking cap on, grabbed his coat, and started stuffing his arms into the sleeves. "We gotta come up with something. You don't think she did it. I don't want to think she did it but, without some solid evidence to the contrary, the system will roll along and I'm sure she'll be convicted and sent to prison."

"I'll call Madison in a while and find out if she wants the class at the house or not."

He sighed. "Yeah. Best you do that, Hon. I'll call you later about dinner."

We kissed and he left.

Sophie nudged me, then walked the couple of steps to where her leash hung from a coat hook by the front door.

"You want to go for a walk?"

Big brown eyes looked sadly into mine. Not the usual response to the "W" word.

I squatted next to her, hugging her around the neck. "Tell ya what, old girl. Mommy will let you out in the yard, then feed you, me, and the kitty girls breakfast, and then you and I will take a walk after the sun comes up."

She leaned into me, giving me a doggy hug, then broke away and headed to the door to the deck to go out.

I checked my Facebook page while I ate my fried egg, deli ham, and Colby-jack cheese sandwich. One thing that caught my eye was an article a friend had posted about a new show at an art gallery in Springfield. They were featuring works, or photos of works they couldn't get hold of, by American artists of the mid-twentieth century whose first names started with the letter "A". I read through the list.

Alice Hardwick, an Illinois-born painter; Arthur Getz, a well known cover illustrator for *New Yorker* magazine; Andreas Feininger, a photographer primarily known for photos he took for *Life* magazine; Armin Landeck, a printmaker well known for his images of New York city; Augusta (Fells) Savage, an African-American sculptor who was part of the Harlem Renaissance in New York City; and Andrew Wyeth, part of the famous Wyeth family of painters.

Of the lot of them, I'm sad to say, Andrew Wyeth was the only one I was familiar with.

I skimmed through posts of banjo jokes, bluegrass jokes, and upcoming festivals and jams from our musical friends. Cat videos. Dog videos. Some chemistry jokes.

An article about a frustrated mathematician also caught my attention. After showing promise in mathematics as a first grader, his parents and teachers had channeled him into advanced mathematics. He was good at it, enjoyed it, and so, went along with their decisions. But, after spending most of his life teaching mathematics and working as a consultant, he had begun to feel that there was something more to his life that he needed to develop and gradually remembered the fun he'd had as a young child playing with crayons and finger paints. He found release and a new purpose in becoming a mathematical artist. He still worked as a mathematics professor while creating noteworthy pieces of art, including a painting entitled "The Golden Ratio" and a pencil drawing in the style of M.C. Escher using regular division of the planes.

An alert beeped.

An email in my Yahoo account. I opened a new tab to see what it was.

It was from Madison.

> *Emory,*
>
> *:-(:-(*
>
> *I know you've heard 'cause I heard Papa call your husband.*
>
> *They took Mama away. She looked so small and miserable. She was shivering when she hugged me.*
>
> *I was going to call you—really want to call you—but I need to say things I don't want anyone in the house to hear.*
>
> *She didn't do it, Emory. Someone either snuck into our house and did it or it had to be Iga or Henri. Why won't they admit it? Why would either of them let Mama go to jail and eventually prison for something she didn't do? I mean, I know she was a handful sometimes but she was usually nice to both of them.*
>
> *They both seem so upset. Iga was crying after Mama was gone. She was in the laundry room, but I heard her. Henri*

made a breakfast none of us really wanted. He looked old and thinner. Pale and fragile. I never would have thought he could look fragile.

Which one of them

Unless neither

No. I can't think that. I won't think that. I don't think that.

It wasn't Mama.

Please. Please don't cancel crochet class. I want everyone to take a turn working on the shawl Mama started. She couldn't take it with her, of course. For obvious reasons a crochet hook is a weapon and so is the yarn. I want us to use the hook you gave her and the yarn Tracy gave her.

I know she can't have the finished shawl either, but I want it ready for her to wrap up in when she gets home.

WHEN she gets home. (No "ifs")

Papa is working from the house but he'll be busy with Mrs. Bogardus, our lawyer, and other people I'm sure. I don't want to be alone and I don't want to go to the hospital and work either. I want to be with you and my crochet class friends.

I'll be looking for everyone a little before 9:00 as always.

Thank you so much,

Hugs

Madison

I just sat there, staring at the screen until a chill slid down my back. Not quite my usual "got-a-knowin'" feeling, but similar. I looked toward the windows to see the deep pink of sunrise easing the purple shadows across the snow-covered back yards. Sophie nudged me. The strange chill passed. I sent a short reply that class was on and I'd see her soon. I closed the computer, put on all my winter garb, hooked Soph to her leash, and we left to take a walk.

Sophie led me along as I imagine a leader dog leads their blind friend, stopping at curbs and nudging me around obstacles. I was too busy thinking to pay much attention to the beauty of the sunny, snow-covered campus like I usually would. At least she kept me on the sidewalks, which were mostly clear of any snow or ice.

I was thinking about the day Theresie Schmid was killed.

Madison and I heard two voices coming from the dining room. I recognized Amy's voice but not Resie's. Madison recognized her voice and that made sense; I didn't know Resie well enough to recognize her voice in a situation like that. So, Resie had to have been alive while Madison and I were in the family room. Madison didn't leave the room and neither did I. As I already knew, we were well accounted for.

We knew Amy was in the dining room. Iga let me into the house, escorted me into the family room then left.

No idea where she went after that. Maybe listening at the hall door into the dining room? Who knows?

I never saw Henri. I assumed he was in his kitchen, which has its own door into the dining room. After all, hadn't I seen him poke his head out of the kitchen door when I was stepping toward Resie's body to find out what had happened?

An image flashed in my mind then trickled like a drip from an icicle down the back of my neck.

Yes! I had seen Henri open the kitchen door and look into the dining room. I'd only given him a glance. A second's time? Less? But now my mind showed me what it had recorded of that moment. Henri hadn't been looking at Resie when he exclaimed, "Oh my God!" He'd been looking at …

The leash slithered out of my hand and Sophie went running off.

It took me a moment to realize where I was and what had happened. I was on the sidewalk that led along the southern edge of West Field and Sophie had taken off into the hedge that marked the edge of the campus property about three yards to the left of the sidewalk.

"Daft dog!" I grumbled. "Sophie! Sophie! Come to Mama so she can smack your behind for running off!"

She was either being a very obstinate doggy or a smart doggy who knew what was waiting for her, because she didn't come. I started through the snow toward the hedge.

"Come on, Soph. Come on. I won't smack your rumpus if you come like a good girl. I just might still smack it if you don't come back now."

The hedge is mostly thick all the way to the ground, but here and there I was catching the flitting gold of my strangely disobedient Golden Retriever.

"Don't turn around and no shouting out, Mrs. Crawford."

The voice and the poke of something into my back occurred simultaneously.

Chapter 22

I STUMBLED ALONG THROUGH THE SNOW. MY KIDNAPPER HAD taken hold of my arm either to make sure I didn't slip and fall or so I couldn't easily run away as we walked westward along the yew hedge.

I hadn't screamed. I hadn't even wet myself when he accosted me.

I had stayed oddly calm, at least on the outside. Inside I was shaking and scared—although …

My kidnapper's tone was polite and his voice gentle when he'd stuck something into my back and told me not to scream. In fact, it had been more a request than an order. He hadn't even been rough when he grasped my arm. Truth be told, I could hardly feel his grip on me at all through my coat sleeve.

Maybe that was why I mostly felt calm.

I wanted information.

"Are you *The Mysterious Red Kidnapper?*"

I hoped using Madison's cute name for him might impress him. I didn't receive an answer.

"You've changed your tactics."

Nothing.

"Someone is apt to see us, even this early. There are a lot of students, profs, too, for that matter, who jog."

"Turn left here," was the only response I received. Enough pressure was applied to my arm to make sure I did as I was told—I had no other plans at the moment anyway. The left turn took us around the end of the hedge and across a short open area.

I decided to quit talking and try to relax my mind; after all, if this was the person who'd kidnapped Tracy, he hadn't hurt her. He hadn't hurt Lilly, though he wasn't with her for very long. Any physical abuse she'd suffered, or had nearly suffered from diving in front of my car, had been because she had run away from him and not because of anything he did to her.

Well, nothing he did to her other than drugging her.

What had Madison said in her emails? Possibly a sad art student?

"Turn left again." My "friend" wasn't very talkative.

We were now heading east, toward town, through a narrow wooded area that runs east and west just south of the Orion Fields neighborhood where Jebbin and I live. We went single file, me in the lead, along a narrow track worn into the undergrowth that would cover the area in the summer, but now was a white stripe running amongst the trees. He wasn't rushing us, which was good since there were tree roots and low spots that I might have tripped over if we were hurrying.

Why hadn't Sophie come back? He hadn't hurt her, had he? No. He'd been behind me or I would have caught glimpses of him the way I'd glimpsed Sophie's golden fur. It was still strange that she hadn't done something to help me.

Come on, brain, I reprimanded myself, back to what Madison had found out. There wasn't much.

A sad, odd art student. Who painted in a realistic manner. Named after some twentieth-century artist.

Why might he be sad? Most art students love to be in class. They're doing what they love. Maybe this student didn't like that he was named after a famous artist? That can be an awkward thing, especially if you're going into the same field as the famous person.

This was making a weird sort of sense.

Tracy is an art major in jewelry and metal sculpture.

Lilly teaches metal sculpture.

Hmm. But the sad student was a painter, Beth had said.

Art.

My escort and I came out of the band of trees, turned right, and walked along College Avenue. He was beside me now, the gun—or whatever it was—poking into my left side. We would look like some young person walking cautiously with an older person in case there were slick spots on the sidewalk. I tried to get a look at his face, but he had the hood on his jacket up. We took a left, crossing College Ave. about half a block down, onto Fern Street. We crossed Louisiana Ave.

The southeast block where Louisiana and Fern crossed had four apartment buildings, each four stories high, that had been built as housing for married students and upperclassmen from

Twombly College.

"Side door," I was told, and we turned at the narrow end of the first building we came to. He slid his keycard and we went inside.

"I know where you live now, you know," I said as we walked up the stairwell with me still in the lead.

"You won't do anything that'll hurt me. You know me. Stop here." He carded the third floor door and held it open for me to go through. He looked at the floor so his face was still hidden. "Three fourteen. Fifth door on the right."

I *know him?*

"*You're not her.*"

The words he'd said to Tracy filled my head, followed by a little voice whispering, "You're her. You'll know what to do."

Before last June I wouldn't have listened to that little voice—the "knowin'" voice. Now I felt I could trust its coaching.

I tried to open my mind and heart to whatever lay ahead of me in his apartment.

Chapter 23

THE APARTMENT'S GREAT ROOM SPACE WAS UNCARPETED BUT most of the living area was covered with an old, heavy, grayish white tarp that, under a lovely large wooden easel that sat to the left of the north-facing plate glass window, was happily splattered with several color wheels worth of paint. Under the small dining table and into the kitchen area, the laminate floor was bare. There was a saggy sofa, a beanbag chair, and a flat panel TV that might actually have been a large computer monitor, and a nice looking speaker dock with an iPod plugged into it.

Then I noticed the art on the walls.

I heard my "knowin'" voice reciting the names from the show at the gallery in Springfield: Alice Hardwick, Arthur Getz, Andreas Feininger, Armin Landeck, Augusta (Fells) Savage, and Andrew Wyeth.

I looked at the pieces of art on the walls. All in the style of Andrew Wyeth. Whose last name sounded like Wyatt. Like old west gambler and deputy sheriff Wyatt Earp—like Beth had mentioned.

"You can sit down, you know." My "host" walked past me into the kitchen and opened the refrigerator. "Would you like a soda? Or I can make us some coffee?"

Now that we were on his turf, he was relaxed and talkative.

I didn't look away from the paintings. Something else was trying to click in my mind. "I should trust anything you give me to drink?"

He chuckled wryly. "That's a fair question, no doubt about it. But yeah, you can. That really didn't work well, anyway, and you came here without making a fuss."

A click in my mind.

"You didn't have a gun or anything, did you?" I still looked at the paintings and pencil drawings, not at him.

"Naw. Sorry I did that, but I didn't think just asking nicely would work."

Puzzle pieces were moving into place in my mind. Click. Click. Like the sound they put in when you do a jigsaw puzzle on a computer. The paintings and drawings had initials in the lower left corners.

W. A.

Like a famous artist but not like. The article about the frustrated mathematician settled itself into place amongst the other parts of the puzzle along with my memory of Mr. Johansen.

A rabbit ran over my grave.

"Not all ghosts are the spirits of the dead."

But maybe this young man was, in some way or other, haunted by the spirit of the deceased artist?

I finally turned around.

"Asking nicely just might have worked, Wyeth. And I'd like a diet soda, if you have diet. If not a regular will do."

He looked at me. Dark wavy hair framed his face. Light colored eyes were topped with the dark brows Lilly had noticed. Joy was lighting a charming smile. "See! I knew it. I knew you'd be my muse come to help me." He grabbed a couple of Diet Dr. Peppers, walked over to me, and handed me one before popping the other one for himself.

I went to the small dining table, set the soda down, and took off my outerwear … thinking as I did so that I was glad he'd said who he thought I was, because if he'd backed me into a corner on it I might have been sunk. That was a puzzle piece I hadn't come up with. I sat down and had a drink of my Dr. Pepper.

"Your muse, eh?" I paused. I fixed what I hoped was an appropriately mystical expression on my face. I tried to look like Aine McAllister looks most of the time. "You need help with figuring out who you are. What you're supposed to do." Another knowin' came to me. "Your heart isn't in your paintings and drawings, is it? That isn't who you really are. You want to work with mathematics."

He stared long and hard at me. "You like red, don't you?"

Ah, yes. Red.

"Wyeth, there's hardly any colors I don't like. But it is true that the warm colors are usually my favorites." A thought popped into my head. "Why did you think Tracy and Professor Comfort were your muse? Neither of them are painters. They both work with metal and sculpting."

"They both like red. They both wear red things fairly often or have red in their artwork. I ..." He looked down at the floor. "I just always imagined my muse as liking red a lot. And ... and doing different kinds of art 'cause a muse is magical and I figured that is why you do lots of things." He looked at me. The sadness Mary's sister Beth had mentioned shadowed his eyes. "I went into the library after the mess up with Professor Comfort, and started looking at the artwork in there. For some reason, I noticed your name on a calligraphy piece and a pencil drawing and a fiber arts thing. And there was a piece of jewelry you'd made in one of the showcases. I didn't know you. I didn't put you together with Dr. Crawford. I asked around and found out who you were and ..."

"Decided I was next?"

He looked away from me. "Sounds awful when you say it flat out like that. I didn't mean it to be awful. I'm just ... lost." He got up and started walking around, occasionally touching a painting or drawing. "Ma always loved Andrew Wyeth's stuff. All the Wyeths, actually. But she didn't have the gift. She sang like a flock of songbirds, she was kind and friendly, and a hard worker, but she never could do artwork. When she had me, she thought it would be fun to name me Wyeth, since her last name was Andrews." He sent a bashful glance my way. "I know. It's corny. Andrew Wyeth— Wyeth Andrews." He went back to walking around. "Anyway, she was over the moon when I started drawing really young. And I was good and I liked making things look real."

Wyeth came and sat across the table from me. For a while he just drank his soda and stared at his hands.

"Then she went and got this crazy idea that I was just like one of the Wyeths. That I should make my stuff look like theirs. Not ..." He looked up in a panic and hastened to add, "Not that it should be exactly like theirs. Not copies where someone might think I was specializing in forgeries. No, just that I should emulate their realism and some of the feelings their work evokes." Wyeth looked back at his hands, the tools of his gift. "And for a while it was cool. I could do it, you know? I was comfortable in their style, put my own twist on it, and I was happy painting."

"But then what?" I gently asked. "You were, what, junior high age? Somewhere in there when mathematics starts replacing arithmetic, and the math started lighting something up inside you. Yes?"

"Yeah!" That lovely look of joy sparked in his eyes again. "Yeah. The math. It's so cool! I mean, it's everywhere. It's in everything. I feel like I'm touching the universe when I'm doing equations. Like I'm part of some immense symphony. I'm inside it all. And, unlike a lot of my arty friends, I was good at math. I took science classes as much as I could, but not as much as I wanted to 'cause Ma would have been hurt if I'd taken extra science instead of using the electives for more art classes."

Wyeth looked around at his walls, at his gallery.

"I loved her. I wasn't angry 'cause she wanted the art, but ... I wished she'd let me have some space for the math and science."

It was a busy morning for grave-runnin' rabbits as another little shiver shook me.

"*Not all ghosts ...*"

No. Not all. He was another soul who wasn't being the person he felt he was born to be.

And yet ...

"You loved her?" I asked. "Past tense?"

"She, ah ... she passed last August. Brain tumor. She, ah ... went fast. She was only in the hospital for a week. I've ... I've sometimes wondered if that was what led to her ending up so obsessed with my being a painter and being so much like the Wyeths. That maybe the tumor affected her that way."

I slipped my hand into his hand that wasn't holding his soda can and gave it a squeeze. "I'm sorry to hear she's gone. The tumor could have done that to her. Brain tumors can cause all sorts of strange reactions. I can tell you really miss her. I know you've been sad since then." I silently thanked Beth for mentioning that the guy in her class had been sadder last semester than he'd been before.

He nodded. He cried a little while. I kept ahold of his hand.

"I know she meant it in a good way, but I was so hoping I could take more science now. You know. She was gone and it wouldn't hurt her if I took the art for fun, for a change of pace from math and science, instead of the other way around." He got up and paced again. "But I found out that she'd been a real miser and had a lot of money stashed in accounts and things. Like she knew she wouldn't be around to take care of me or something." He looked at me. "I thought I was here at Twombly all on grants and scholarships." His lips trembled and he was getting more agitated. "But—oh man, it's a huge 'but'—then I found out she'd paid for the apartment so I'd have room for a studio. I've been in here since second semester of my freshman year. She finagled it somehow. You know, it's only supposed to be upper-class students and married students here. She paid for all my art supplies and my food—both at the college cafeteria and here. And I've come to find out she covered about half the tuition too."

He went silent.
Paced.
Kicked the beanbag chair.
Paced.
Ran his hands through his hair.

"I don't want to be angry with her, I really don't; but she made a will and it stipulates that the money for school stops if I change my major, and I won't get my inheritance unless I graduate with a fine arts major. Everything will continue if I stay at Twombly and stay in art, but if I don't, I'm on my own."

He sat down across from me again.

"For all that she was such a hard worker, she never let me have a job. I did art. Well, and normal fun kid stuff. I mean it wasn't like I didn't do Little League and stuff like that, 'cause I did. But she wouldn't let me get a job. She always said, 'Art will be your job. Why do anything else?' and I never argued."

Both his hands encircled mine.

"I'm terrified I won't be able to work a job and go to school. And I'm scared because I'm wanting to do math and I don't know how to work a job and I don't want to lose my inheritance. The art isn't what it used to be to me, but at least I still enjoy that I do it well. You know, profs and people really like my stuff. I think if I could do more math and science the art would be soothing. Now it feels like a prison."

A frightened little boy's eyes pleaded with me.

"She went away. My Ma was my muse. She loved me, inspired me, encouraged me. I painted and drew for her because she loved it so. My muse left and now I can't paint. Can't draw. Can't do math either. I'm losing my mind, I think. The idea came to me that maybe my muse had moved into someone else. That she'd want to stay close by."

Tears rolled down my face and Wyeth's.

"Help me, Mrs. Crawford. Help bring my muse back to me and tell me what I should do."

Chapter 24

IT PROBABLY WORRIED WYETH THAT I WAS TAKING SO LONG TO reply, but I knew we'd reached a point in this discussion where I'd have to be careful with what I said and how I said it.

"Bring your muse back? Are you meaning bring your mother back?"

He leaned back, both hands raised as if to push me away. "No! Like, oh my God, no! No. I'm not that nutty. No. No zombie Ma or ghost Ma or ... whatever sort of spooky weird things they make movies about." Wyeth's eyelids relaxed. He took a deep breath, shuddered, then continued. "Whew! Yeah. I guess I can see where I sounded like that." He got back up to pace again. "I mean, I didn't even mean that you, like, have some ethereal 'Ma-muse spirit thing' living inside you or some ghosty thing like that."

It was my turn to be patient as he took a while to speak again.

"Ah. Yeah. I mean … I sorta meant that someone would show up to be my inspiration. Ah … you know. Be my cheerleader, like my Ma always was." He stopped and looked at me. "Except, hopefully, be able to cheer for the math and science, too." He came back to the table and flopped into his chair. "I've made a major mess of all this, haven't I?"

The pleading look was back, but now I had a good opening for what I needed to say to him.

"Hate to say it," I said as soothingly as I could, "but—yeah. It's a big mess." I took hold of his hand again. "You asked me to help, like a mom would help. I'm good at that because I'm a mom whose grown-up kids still like her and want to be around her. I get mothering."

We both grinned at that.

"First," I said, reaching behind me to dig in my coat pocket. "We need to make some phone calls."

My phone rang.

"May I?"

Wyeth nodded.

It was Jairus.

"Hello, Jairus."

"Hi, Emory. Are you okay? Sophie showed up on our front porch barking her head off."

"Yes, I'm fine. I was just going to call you, in fact."

"I know." I could hear the smile in his voice. "I think Sophie's barking brought my gift back from vacation. You're with the kidnapper, aren't you?"

I was sure he could hear the smile in my voice equally well.

"Indeed I am, and all is well. We could use for you to send over your lawyer and …" I spoke to Wyeth, "Who's your academic counselor at the college?"

"Mr. Patterson."

Back to Jairus I said, "Mrs. Bogardus and George Patterson from the art department. He's Wyeth Andrews' counselor."

"Uh huh. W-y-e-t-h A-n-d-r-e-w-s." He said the name slowly and I could tell he was writing it down. "I woke up this morning from a dream where I kept seeing the letters W A all over the place. I guess my gift was making its way back before Sophie got here. I'll call Simone and George and get them both over there. You're at the Fern St. Apartments, aren't you."

"Yes. Building A, apartment three fourteen. And Jairus?"

"Yes?"

"Tell Madison to let the crochet class know I'll be late, but I will be there."

"I will. She's been worried about you."

"She's a sweetie. I'll stay here until George or Simone gets here and probably a bit longer. I want to make sure Wyeth is comfortable before I leave."

"Okay, Emory. Thank you."

"And thank you, Jairus. Bye."

"Bye."

I explained to Wyeth who all was going to be showing up. That he might have to go to the police station but that he shouldn't have to be there long as, hopefully, Mrs. Bogardus could get him out on bail. And, if Tracy and her family and Professor Comfort could be persuaded to not press charges, he might not even have to go through a trial, though he might have to have counseling and maybe some community service to do. Then I asked him if I could call my husband and let him know I was okay and that the case of The Mysterious Red Kidnapper had been solved.

"Sure." He smiled and even chuckled. "I sound like a Sherlock Holmes story."

"Yes, you do. Maybe a lit major will write it up for you." I winked.

After calling Jebbin, who made several "Miss Marple" and "Nancy Drew" comments, I let Wyeth know what I was hoping we could do for him.

"We'll get Mr. Patterson busy setting up a new schedule for you for spring semester. One that will put you on a track for a fine arts major with a minor in straight mathematics or one of the sciences. Whichever you'd like. Eventually, you may need to take another year's worth of math after you graduate, and you should be able to go on and do graduate work in mathematics if you want to. Then we'll also ask Mrs. Bogardus to look into your mother's will, your trust, and everything to make sure we can open the doors to the math and science without any risk to your financial support."

Wyeth jumped up, rushed to my side of the table, picked me up off my chair, and danced me around his living room. Not a simple thing, seeing as I'm sure I weigh twenty to thirty pounds more than he does.

"You are a mother muse! You are a mother muse!" he shouted several times before setting me down.

We sat back down at the table. I lifted my Dr. Pepper can.

"To math, and science, and art, and the fact that they can all live harmoniously together."

"And to miracles." Wyeth added as we tunked the cans together and drank.

Chapter 25

I WAS AN HOUR AND A HALF LATE FOR CROCHET CLASS, STANDING at the foot of the front steps of Cornelia House, wondering what awaited me inside. My "knowin'" gift was working over time today and I just had the eeriest feeling about being in the house.

I'd gone home first, as I hadn't taken my walk with my crocheting supplies with me. Someone had brought Sophie home. She looked rather pleased with herself, as though she'd been in cahoots with the Lord in leading my gift and I to where Wyeth could find me. I gave her a treat, then gave Hortense and Kumquat treats too as they sensed Sophie was getting food and they refused to be left out, told Sophie she was a good girl for going to tell Jairus there was a problem, gathered up my things, and left.

Iga let me in—eliciting no particular special feelings on my part. She had obviously been crying. She was obviously still keeping a tight rein on herself when she had to be around other people.

"Madison will be so glad you're here, Mrs. Crawford."

I barely heard her. I turned to see fresh tears pooling in her grateful, though red, eyes.

"Everyone is here." She gestured across the entryway. "They're in the parlor, as usual."

The question bombardment began as soon as everyone finished saying how glad they were that I'd finally arrived.

"Were you really with the kidnapper?"

"Did you hit him with your car?" That from Ed, along with a devilish wink.

"Has he been arrested?"

"Did he drug you, too?"

"Where were you? Did he break into your house?"

"Did you see what he looks like?"

That last whispered question brought all the other questions to a halt.

"Yes," I answered Tracy. "Yes, I saw his face. I know his name and I spent quite a bit of time talking to him." I looked around at the faces around me, all eager for information. "Let's sit down. You can all pick up your crocheting and I'll talk while you work."

I told them the whole story, oddly without a single interruption from the usually talkative group.

"So," I said, closing up my tale, "I think everything will end well for Wyeth, and for Lilly Comfort, and you, Tracy."

Tracy looked up from her crocheting. I noticed that she and Suzanne had sat on either side of Madison. The pair had turned into the class comforters. "Oh yes, Emory! I mean, I was horribly scared, and not being able to remember much to help the police out didn't help either. But I totally feel better about it now. Knowing Wyeth was so sad and scared himself, and he didn't hurt me. Never would have hurt me. Well … yeah, I feel a lot better. I'm sure I'll still have some bad dreams about it but what you've learned from him really helps. I'm glad you could be a mom to him like you were to me after he let me go." She huffed a wry laugh. "He should have come to you first. Did he ever say why he left all those red things in the girls' rooms, or why he took me?"

"Not about the red gifts, no. He didn't say and I didn't think to ask him about that. Otherwise, he just said that he always felt his muse liked red and that he'd noticed you, and Professor Comfort, both seemed to like red."

"I'm so glad it's all gotten settled out." Naomi nodded. "I know how much of a difference it makes when you have answers. I'll always feel badly about Dr. Dawson, sorry he was killed like he was, but it helps that you figured out who did it, Emory, and that she explained her motives."

A rumble interrupted the conversation.

We all looked at Carrie, who blushed.

"My stomach always knows when it lunch time."

Everyone laughed. We had been so involved with my news that we hadn't even heard Henri setting out the lunch buffet. But then, I think, that is part of a good chef's training, to set up without disrupting the event.

"One thing, Emory, before we head over to the buffet," Carrie went on. "I would like to meet Wyeth. Help him meet some of us math and science geeks … If you think that would help?"

I stood and the group followed suit and we headed to the buffet table at the end of the room by the door into the kitchen. I stepped up beside Carrie. "I think that's a wonderful idea, Carrie. Maybe the three of us can do lunch or something when everything about his situation has gotten settled out."

I was getting seconds ... Not a huge amount of seconds, but I'd had a stressful morning and felt in need of fortification. At any rate, I was having a few more tastes of my favorites amongst Henri's offerings when I looked up to see him peeking around the edge of the door that opened into the butler's pantry and the kitchen. He looked gaunt, pasty ... haunted.

And I shivered.

Yep. Spine tingle and everything.

And in my mind I heard myself telling Iga to get Amy and Madison away. I was staring at a dead body on a parquet floor. Hearing Henri's gasped exclamation of "Oh, my God!" Looking up and seeing him ...

Peeking around a door.

Looking into a room where a dead woman was lying on the floor in plain sight.

Yet he wasn't looking at Resie. He said "Oh, my God!" looking at the backs of Amy, Madison, and Iga as they hurried from the room.

And then the vision faded and I was staring at Henri, peeking around the butler's door in Cornelia House.

"I was just checking to see if anything needs to be refilled," he said, returning what must have been the strange look I was surely giving to him.

I shook my head to clear my thoughts and, I hoped, my expression. "Ah ... of course." I looked up and down the table. "Um.

Looks like that fantastic ham and pasta salad is about gone. The chili looks half gone. Ah …"

He came into the parlor, wearing what should have been a smile but wasn't cheery enough to be called that. "That's okay, Mrs. Crawford. I'll come around and look for myself. I know what has probably run its course and what things people might want more of."

"Of course." I turned to where the class was sitting by the middle of the long room's two fireplaces. "Hey everyone!" They all looked over. "How about a round of applause and thanks for all the wonderful food Henri has been supplying us with?"

Cheers and applause rang out, as well as bringing everyone back over to the table to catch a few more nibbles.

Henri looked shocked then blushed and smiled a genuine smile. "You are all very gracious. It is my pleasure to feed …" His words caught for a moment. "To feed Mrs. Twombly and Miss Madison's friends." After an awkward little bow, he took a swift spin around the table before retreating to his kitchen.

I needed to talk to Madison. I gestured Madison over while the others continued to fill up their corners from the food table or headed for the hall where the restrooms were.

"You and I …"

"Need to talk to Henri," she finished for me.

Chapter 26

WE STARED AT EACH OTHER FOR A MOMENT BEFORE MADISON broke off to stare at her feet, which she shuffled back and forth as though trying to get a better look at her shoes.

"I'm starting to get the Twombly giftedness." The words were quiet but strong. "Papa hasn't told me anything to the effect, but I think you have some giftedness, too." She looked up at me, challenging me with her eyes. "You do, don't you?"

"Yes, and Jairus knows about it."

Madison nodded, keeping her attention fixed on me. "Okay. That's out of the way. I've been having the creepy-crawlies ever since I hit send on that email this morning."

She looked away and stamped her foot before using it to kick at the leg of a chair near her. "This whole thing stinks! It worse than stinks."

Ed ambled by us and we realized we were in the traffic pattern. We moved over by a wall.

"I try not to cuss much," Madison went on. "I just don't like how it sounds and feels when I'm around kids that do it all the time, so I try to avoid it. Not that I'm trying to be a goody-goody, it just isn't my thing. But this morning after that snake in the grass deputy sheriff took my Mama, I went upstairs, punched my pillow, and said every single cuss word I've ever heard." Her arms had wrapped around her like a defensive force field. She started chewing at her lower lip and her nostrils flared. "But later …" She sniffed, pulled in a large breath through her nose, blew it out in a huff, and seemed to gather herself somewhat. "Later this morning, Papa seemed to be doing better." She looked back at me. "His vibe has felt off lately. I know that sounds über-spacey but I know you know what I mean. Something about him has been off and I think it had something to do with the gift."

"Yes. He told me about it. I saw him in the Japanese Garden, Saturday evening."

She gave a curt nod. "Cool. I'm glad he told someone. We … ah, we don't share that much about it. I mean we do, but not like that. Whatever I mean by that." She waved her hand as if she was backhanding a fly. "So, yeah. I think it's coming back. He, you know, feels better. Anyway, that email I sent and the stuff you sent that your friend researched for you. It was like Henri's name was vibrating. I could feel his name like a bell not ringing true. Off pitch." Again, I got that intense look from her. "I think Henri killed Resie. But it's not like that's real evidence or anything. And then, I start to think maybe it's just that I want it to be anyone other than my Mama."

I nodded slowly, trying to be a calming influence. "Totally understandable, Madison. That said, I think he did it, too. Same sort of thing, though. Not anything we can use to convince the authorities that he did it instead of your mom."

I thought for a few moments.

"It's a shame we can't find out what he was working on in the kitchen that afternoon, you know, what he was prepping for dinner. We might have something solid if we did. I don't know that anyone in the household actually had dinner that night, but he wouldn't have known that ahead of time, even if he did kill her. He would have been prepping dinner before it happened. Then we all got gathered up and questioned at the house, Henri and Iga included, so that interrupted his preparations. Then we all got taken off to the station for further interrogation. But I can't imagine that Henri would have fixed a big meal when you got home, as it was late and I doubt anyone was hungry, including him. But, then again, I hadn't really thought about it until now. We really do need to find out what he was originally planning for dinner that night and what kinds of prep work it needed."

MaddyHatter looked like The Cheshire Cat.

"He keeps a food and menu diary in the kitchen. Writes down everything we all have every day, well, what he prepares for us at least, even if it's just one of us asking him to make a snack. If he makes it, he writes it down."

"Where does he keep it?"

"There's a small desk-nook area even in this house's kitchen for the chef to work at. He keeps it there, out in the open, on top of the desk next to his laptop."

"So …" I'm sure I had my own sly grin going. "Instead of talking to him, this might be a good time for you to visit the kitchen to just sort of walk around and open cupboards and drawers and stuff like a normal idle teenager."

"Okay. And ..."

"Is it a big notebook?"

"No. It's a pocket-sized moleskin. Are you suggesting ...?"

"How are your pickpocketing skills?"

Chapter 27

THE REST OF THE AFTERNOON, MADISON WAS RESTLESS. SHE would crochet a bit. Walk around the parlor a bit. Leave the room and come back. No one questioned it—we all knew she was having a terrible day tacked onto an awful week.

Everyone was gone by one-thirty.

Madison told her dad that I had invited her to Fill Your Cup for a fancy dessert and the beverage of her choice, and we left too.

Mid-afternoon wasn't a busy time for the coffee shop. The booth in the back corner was as secluded as a desert island. My tiramisu melted in my mouth, the mellow hazelnut latte was … mellow. Madison had already drunk half of her caramel hot cocoa and eaten three quarters of her triple chocolate brownie with whipped cream.

And we'd found what we needed in the little moleskin book.

"Is he going to miss this very quickly?" I asked.

"Well, I don't know for sure." Madison flipped through the pages. "But, tonight's dinner is already ... well, the original, which was a regular type dinner, is crossed out. "Assorted Sandwich Platter, Deli Salads, Corn chips, Potato chips" is written in, so yeah, tonight's dinner is already written in, so I doubt Henri would be writing in it anymore today."

My Artful Dodger smiled at me.

"And, seeing as I found a new blank book in the desk drawer that he must have brought from home, since this one is nearly finished, and switched it out with this one ... I doubt he'll notice it any time soon."

I smiled and shook my head. "You worry me with how good you are at all this snooping around."

"A brilliant mind is a terrible thing to waste." She winked. "That and I've grown up in a home with all sorts of interesting people coming and going, meetings with city and college muckity-mucks going on behind closed doors. Considerably older siblings doing all the interesting things older siblings do. Yeah. I've become adept at espionage, but I refuse to be turned to the Dark Side."

I held out my hand for the book, which Madison handed over with a triumphant smile. I turned again to last Sunday's entry.

"The timing is perfect. He would have been getting things ready to cook dinner about the time ... it happened."

Madison's mood dropped from its high of a moment ago.

"Yeah. Yeah he would have been."

"Shall we go back to Cornelia House? I don't think we can sit on this and I don't want you to be tempted to talk to him alone."

We both sighed. The air in the coffee shop was suddenly heavy as a fog, even though everything else had gotten clearer.

"Yes. Let's go."

Chapter 28

JAIRUS CAME INTO THE MAIN HALL AS MADISON AND I WERE removing our coats by the front door.

"You're going to talk to Henri?"

We all looked at each other. Jairus' intuition was back in full force.

"Yes," Madison replied before me. "We actually have tangible proof." She held up the moleskin notebook. "It's in his food diary."

Her father nodded and waved us to follow him as he turned to head into the kitchen.

I don't know what we all looked like to Henri, but I'm sure it wasn't anything pleasant. He was sitting on a stool at the work island in the middle of the kitchen looking as if he'd already seen the end. An envelope and some handwritten sheets of tri-folded paper lay on the shining granite surface.

"We know," was all Jairus said.

Henri nodded. He'd already been crying. "I was …" He sniffed. Took a few deep breaths, then continued. "I was going to confess. Mrs. Amy shouldn't have to spend another night in a jail because of me." He gestured at the papers. "I'd already decided, but then Iga brought this to me and … she went to the house. Captain Schneider called and said the techs were finished and someone could go to the house if they wished to begin the cleanup. She didn't go into the dining room, said she figured a professional cleaning service would need to do that room, so she went to clean out Miss Schmid's room. This," he waved his hand over the papers, "was on her desk in the envelope, addressed to me."

My mind showed me Mr. Johansen. My mind said, *Not all ghosts are the spirits of the dead—but some are that as well.*

"You knew her, didn't you? Before you were Henri Boulanger? You knew her in New York."

He gasped. Choked. Madison got him a glass of water. Jairus was at his side.

"How did you know?" he asked when he could speak again.

"I've put together information. Clues? I guess. Things I've heard and things I remember from my childhood. Things a friend researched for me. Neither of you had a past that could be found. So the thought arises, perhaps changed identities? I …"

My eyes closed as I thought again of sad Mr. Johansen. Of sad Wyeth Andrews. Of Amy who also seemed to have popped up from nowhere.

"I knew a man when I was a girl who, when he died and my father—his pastor—tried to find his family and ended up finding out that that man, Mr. Johansen, had started out being Mr. Knutzen. He'd been an abusive husband who'd abandoned his wife and child. They died because he'd abandoned them, and when he heard, he decided he had to leave behind the man he'd been, start over, and apologize to them the only way he could think of. By becoming a good man, a caring man."

"Did he?" Henri whispered.

"Yes. He became a good Christian man, beloved by the whole small town he'd moved to. He became a wonderful husband and father. His wife had already passed and his kids all lived far away when he was dying. By the time they would get there, he knew he'd be gone. So, he told my father the whole story from his deathbed, asking that he tell no one. My dad didn't tell me until many years later."

Henri closed his eyes. He looked infinitely weary.

"Different," he sighed. "Different but the same results. Yes. I was Elmer Nordstrom and she was Sally Bosch, a nanny type person who ..." Tears flowed and dripped onto the granite. "She killed my son."

Madison gasped. Jairus and I sank onto two of the other stools around the island.

None of us had expected this.

"She was acquitted. I hated her because I knew she'd gotten away with murdering my little boy. I'd ... I'd lost his mother, my sweetheart, my Patty, when she was only twenty." Henri took a drink of water from the glass Madison had gotten him earlier. "Brain aneurism. I was a short-order cook at a local diner and couldn't quit to be home with Daniel."

He got up to go stir whatever was in the stockpot on the stove and take a taste. Nodding his approval, he came back to the counter, but didn't sit down. He got a dishcloth, a bottle of cleaner, and started wiping down the granite.

"After they let her go I just had to get out of there. I was so full of hate. Anger. I'd started drinking too much and I feared I'd drink myself to death with it. I had always dreamed of being a 'real' chef, one with training who could work in fine restaurants. My boss at the diner and a few of the regulars got together the money to get me started at Le Cordon Bleu. I chose to go to the branch in Ottawa 'cause I had to get away from New York. One of my friends was … well, not a very law abiding man. I'll just say that. I told him I wanted to disappear when I left, so he arranged for all the papers I'd need. One of the early and important chefs at the original Le Cordon Bleu in Paris was Chef Henri-Paul Pellaprat. I took his first name and boulanger, the French word for baker, and became Henri Boulanger." Henri threw the cloth into the sink, sank wearily onto the stool he'd vacated earlier, and started drawing random squiggles on the counter top with his right index finger. His eyes followed his finger. "How'd you figure it out?"

Madison set his diary on the counter. "It's in here."

"My husband and the other forensic scientist who's working with him told me they found olive oil on the crochet hook, which made sense to me as Amy had told me that's what she cleaned it with. But, they said it was a thicker layer than they would have expected on the body of the hook, and it had spices in it. Rosemary, sage, and garlic. You had done like any good chef would do."

I reached over and opened the book to that Sunday's page.

"You planned to serve the sage and rosemary olive oil dip at lunch, making up a larger batch than you'd need, and using the extra to make the sage, rosemary, and garlic rub for the steak at dinner. Amy might have had the mix for the dip on her hands, although no one would leave a thickish coating like that on their hands, but she wouldn't have had the garlic because that was added later. You left thick and thin areas of oil but no prints because of the folds in the vinyl gloves you were wearing."

Henri nodded his bowed head. "Yes. Yes, that's it. I was rubbing the herbed oil into the steaks. I heard Sally—now Resie the personal assistant—and Amy arguing. We all knew how Resie was behaving. Well, we all suspected why she was here to begin with, but that was Mr. Jairus' business. Anyway, that was the last straw for me. I knew who she was, what she'd done, and here she was ruining someone else's life. Someone I liked. Amy was always kind to me, as if she understood about being a working person. Like she could tell I'd … I'd had a terrible hurt. And there was that horrible bitch, Sally, cutting in on my family again. I went into the dining room when I heard the doors into the family slam together. Sally was picking up the broken porcelain from the vase."

His searching eyes sought each of us out.

"Do you know how much venom you can put into a whisper? Yeah, I see you all do. I gave her hell without any of you hearing. She just stood there, gaping at me like she'd never heard about it or something. I put my hand on the table. Right on top of that crochet hook. I hadn't seen it there. It sorta blended into the wood of the tabletop. But it was in my hand and her eyes had this strange blank look."

He drank the rest of the water, held the glass out for more. Jairus got it for him. He drank it dry in one long gulp.

"If my hand had been empty, she'd still be alive, but that hook was in it and it went into her eye and … and …" Henri shook with sobs. "I … I felt a weird crunchy sort of pop. She … gasped … a little tiny breath of a gasp and started to fall over. She … she must have hit her head on the planter or gotten a shard of the vase in her head or something 'cause she didn't scream or move again or anything, and I was so scared. I always thought it'd feel good to kill her. To pay her back for letting Daniel choke to death. But it didn't. I went into the kitchen and into the little half bath in there, and threw up. I … I came out and heard Mrs. Amy screaming. I ran to the door and …"

The words had gushed out of him, pouring from the wounds of his past and what he had done.

His bloodshot eyes stared into space. They were the only things on his face with any color in them. I was certain, in his mind, he was seeing the swinging door at the Twombly mansion that led from his beloved kitchen into the dining room.

"She'd seen it. Mrs. Amy and her little girl had found her and had to see that. And …"

He turned to Madison, arms stretched out to her and she stepped into his hug.

"I'm so sorry, Madison girl."

Jairus joined them. I got off my stool and walked to the far end of the kitchen.

Eventually I heard Jairus.

"We have to tell the authorities, Henri. You know we do."

The big man nodded.

He patted the papers on the desk.

"I think Sally's reaction, that weird blank look that angered me, was disbelief because she knew she'd written this. Shock that it was all falling in before she'd had the chance to give the letter to me. It … doesn't change what happened. She was negligent when my boy died but I think she should have admitted it, back then. She should have called 911 or something. But … well, it's all in there. I … don't have anything more to say except I'm so sorry. I didn't do any better than she did."

Jairus left the room to call Captain Henry.

I called Jebbin to briefly fill him in and suggest that he and Chatty order pizza for themselves.

Chapter 29

JAIRUS, MADISON, HENRI, AND I, ALONG WITH THE FOOD DIARY and Theresie Schmid's letter, went in Jairus' car to the station.

Henri went in. A couple of hours later, Amy came out.

While we'd waited for everyone to decide that they could release Amy, I had called Jebbin to fully fill him in on everything that had happened to me today.

The Twomblys dropped me off at my car near Cornelia house when they picked up Iga to go out for dinner. The stockpot of chili Henri had simmering on the stove for dinner had been put in the refrigerator before we left Cornelia House for the station. They knew they weren't going to want it tonight.

Chatty and Jebbin were sitting at the kitchen table when I got home. They had managed to leave me a couple slices of pizza.

"Okay," Jebbin said after I got settled at the table. "You need to explain to us how you and a teenaged girl managed to solve two crimes in one day."

"Jealous?" I teased.

"No," Chatty replied, though the comment had been aimed at Jebbin. "No, we are not jealous. We are ... what is that term I have heard? Ah, yes! We are flabbergasted."

"That's okay, then. So am I." Time out for a bite of pizza, a sip of diet Vernors, and I was ready to spill the beans. "I can hardly claim too much credit for solving the kidnapping. Madison's information from her confidential sources did a lot for that case."

"Oooooh! 'Confidential sources.' 'That case,'" Jebbin scoffed, then smiled at me. "What do you think, Chatty? Isn't she just sounding all professional now? Are you and 'Nancy' going to hang out a shingle?"

"Oh my, yes! Most professional," Chatty agreed with a sly smile. "I will do your forensic work for you, Mrs. Crawford. My colleague here seems to not be taking your endeavor seriously. *I* will treat you and Miss Twombly most professionally."

I did my best mock shock expression, then laughed. "No. No shingle. No aspirations of careers. Not right now, at any rate." Turning to Chatty, I added, "Thank you for your generosity, Dr. Chatterjee. Your offer will be the first my partner and I consider, *if* we decide to pursue our obvious gifts in this field." I paused and thought while Chatty beamed and stuck out his tongue at Jebbin. "Well," I continued. "Speaking for myself, I've no career plans, but who knows what Madison might decide to do. Anyway, I had a lot of help solving that case ..." I looked pointedly at Jebbin. "... since Wyeth kidnapped me. Madison had gotten some clues that probably would have produced him as a suspect eventually, but it was hardly detective work on my part when the boy walks off with me."

"Good point, good point," Jebbin admitted as I ate more pizza. "I'll cut you some slack on that one, but what about the murder? You were a bit confusing over the phone. Did Henri confess first, or did you figure it out first?"

"That was mostly good detective work, otherwise known as nosiness, on the part of Madison and me. But even you two suspected him. You guys couldn't help it that Captain Henry Schneider was being even more uncooperative than usual and was doing his best to not accept anyone but Amy as the murderer."

"True," Jebbin admitted. "We are saddled with having to go through proper channels."

I patted his hand. "Sorry. Madison and I can square dance outside the square. But even then, we have to have something that will stand up as proper evidence when all is said and done. And you two ..." I gestured to include Chatty. "You guys provided the forensic evidence about the olive oil that led to the evidence in the food diary that backed it up."

"True," Jebbin repeated.

After that, we discussed our children, the weather, and how well the Twombly Stallions ice hockey team was doing. After a while, Chatty bid us farewell. He was heading to his hotel for the night and then home to East St. Louis first thing in the morning.

I got up and threw the empty pizza box and dirty paper plates in the trash, then sat back down at the table.

"Are you mad at me?" I asked my unusually quiet husband.

He didn't answer as quickly as I would have liked.

"No. Not mad. Not sure what I am, but not mad."

Sophie *clickety-clicked* into the kitchen to get a drink. Kumquat and Hortense levitated to the tabletop and made themselves comfortable on the two empty placemats.

I waited for Jebbin to figure his feelings out.

"Mystified."

"Mystified?"

"Yeah. Best I'm coming up with. I mean, you've always liked mystery stories and cop shows. Forensics has always interested you. But … well … you just never got involved before."

Jebbin took hold of my hand and we looked at each other.

"I don't mind. Mostly. It's just …" He looked down at our hands. "I never saw this coming. You teaching crocheting and knitting and the like, yeah. That I saw. But you morphing into an amateur sleuth, I didn't see."

His other hand joined the first in cradling my hand.

There were tears in his eyes when he looked up at me.

"I'm worried. Scared. Last time, you could've been shot by Cameron. This time you get kidnapped."

We sat in silence for a moment as his words sank in.

We both looked at our hands.

"You want me to resist the temptation to get involved? I mean … I've never sought it out. The situations just seem to get thrust upon me. Wrong place. Wrong time."

"I don't know. I don't think I can keep you from … what you said is right. It's not like you're checking the police report column of the paper every day so you can go snooping. It just … happens."

"Yes. It does. Doesn't mean it will again, you know."

"I suppose. Twice doesn't a pattern make. Still … promise me you won't go sneaking off and not telling me what you're up to? Let me know you're …"

He squeezed my hands and I looked up to see my favorite

mischievous glint in his eyes.

"Let me know you're on a 'case'?"

"You'll always know—" I grinned. "As soon as I do."

He nodded. "Settled."

"Settled," I agreed.

He looked at the clock on the kitchen wall. "Nine o'clock. Watch something off Netflix and cuddle on the couch with the fireplace going, Mrs. Crawford?"

"You're on, Mr. Crawford."

It was the last day of the crochet class. We were back at my house, in my cozy lower level family room, and everyone had been having a wonderful time.

Until a suitable new chef for the Twomblys could be found, Fiorello Guido, the head chef at the college, was taking care of the Twombly family and Iga. Amy had asked him if he could supply a lunch buffet for us and he'd done so with his usual flare and exquisite cooking. The desserts were easy to decide, I'm sure. He knew my love of tiramisu, and everyone's love of his Dark Chocolate-Cherry Cake with real, fresh whipped cream to top it off. Sandwiches made with meats he brought and carved fresh, piled onto his fabulous multi-grain bread with a variety of sandwich toppings and condiments. And seven different kinds of salads.

Everyone showed off their projects. A few had done more than one.

Carrie had made five shawls in different colors, one for herself, her mother, and her three sisters. They were triangular shaped, done by never making the second corner in the pattern that turns the work into either a square or a rectangle.

Madison had finished her green and gold Twombly college scarf, which she had made long enough that the ends were down to her knees.

Naomi had invited Aine to come and enjoy lunch with us, and to model the shawl she had made for her florist shop mentor.

Tom had sent off the baby afghan he'd made for his soon-to-arrive nephew but was wearing his Twombly scarf loosely draped over his shoulders.

Ed was sharing his huge Twombly colors afghan with Sophie, Hortense, and Kumquat. The furry kids were all sound asleep on it.

Tracy, her mother, and her grandmother had finished the rainbow pastels afghan they had started while she was in the hospital after Wyeth had kidnapped her. She went back to working on the scarf she had started with and had given it to Wyeth. He'd apologized to her and Lilly Comfort with genuine sincerity, and she wanted to let him know she'd forgiven him.

Suzanne's crocheted "quilt" of pastel to bold colored four inch squares in a rainbow order pattern was a work of art—and her art teacher proved it by giving her college credits for it as an independent study.

Marge was still working on her pastel Twombly colors afghan, but it was looking lovely. Her arthritis kept her from working on it as much as she would have liked. And there weren't any stains left on it from its brief stint of pillowing Lilly's head.

The class had finished Amy's shawl, the one that she had started when she returned to the class, and she refused to take it off even though it was warm in the family room. But she had another surprise in store.

"If I could have everyone's attention," Madison called out after we were all sitting around, letting our lunch settle. "Mama, will you come stand by me?"

Amy looked embarrassed at being put front and center—something I never thought I'd see.

"Mama," Madison began. "I was so happy when we started this class together. The together part being the happiest part. There was a lot of weird stuff happening and it was good for you and me to get away from the house together."

Madison turned to get something out of her tote bag. Her Mom stood there, still looking awkward.

"Actually, I need you up here, too, Emory." She deftly kept what she'd retrieved out of sight.

I walked over and stood on the other side of Amy.

"Mama, I was so proud of you when you came back to the class. I'd been having fun learning to crochet with you and working on our projects together in the evenings. We'd talk about yarn we'd seen online or in the knitting magazines I'd found at the library. I was so relieved when you came back."

The class surprised us all by applauding.

When they quieted down, Madison continued.

"I've done something that I hope you won't mind. Papa thought it was a great idea and paid for it all." She turned to look at her classmates. "First, I want to tell you all that you're each getting a yellow Furls Candy Shop hook like mine."

Everyone gasped then started saying thank you all at once.

After saying "You're welcome," several times, she grinned and waggled her eyebrows. "Hey, what good is having money if you don't buy goodies for friends?"

A round of laughter and more thanks ensued, ending when

she brought small black boxes out from behind her back.

Madison looked at her Mom. "I know you lost your Furls hook, and I hope you'll accept this. If you … if it … if I was wrong and this bothers you, we'll send them back."

Amy took the box Madison held out to her tentatively, as though it might hurt her hand.

"Don't open it yet, Mama." She held out a box to me. "You've been so good to Tracy, to Mama, Papa, and me. You've even been good to Wyeth. If you hadn't taught this class a lot of good things might not have happened. This is for you with a lot of love and thanks."

I took my box.

Madison held the other one up and waved it over her head with a big smile on her face.

"This one's for me because I wanted one too."

Everyone laughed.

"Inside these boxes," she continued. "Are olive wood Furls hooks. Olive trees, olive branches, and olive wood have been a symbol of peace for many ages, and that's what these are to me. I've found peace and relaxation when I'm crocheting. It helped when I was so worried about my Mama, and Papa, and myself. And I love thinking about what this class and crocheting have done for my Mama and me." Madison looked around the room at everyone. "And all the friends it's brought us." She looked at her mother. "I hope the olive wood will help you to think of this too. Go ahead and open them up."

The hooks were beautiful. So very different in appearance than the exotic Bloodwood had been. I picked mine up. The wood seemed invitingly warm to the touch.

"I hardly know how to thank you, Madison," I whispered as

my throat tightened up and my eyes got teary.

Amy had lifted hers from the box as well. Tears dripped off her nose as she looked down at it in her hand.

Softly, Madison said, "I got a larger size. They're size 'L' like my Candy Shop hook. It's a good size for all the funky, cool yarns you liked in the magazines, Mama."

Amy didn't say a word …

She just turned and hugged her daughter and cried.

THE END

Resie's Letter

DEAR HENRI (ELMER),

I hardly know where to begin—how to start to say all I need to say.

I didn't recognize you until yesterday. I usually have had no need to go into the kitchen, but yesterday it seemed a good place to get away from the family for a while and have a cup of coffee. You ignored me, which gave me plenty of time to watch you. You still have your habit of resting your index finger between your upper lip and your nose when you're thinking. I understood then why your voice had sounded familiar and your eyes reminded me of someone.

Not meaning this to be rude, though I know it will most likely sound it, but you've changed a lot, physically, since I worked for you in 1991. You were actually too thin back then. You didn't eat much because you were still mourning Patty and were working so many hours that you wore what little you did eat off. Now you look like that chef on TV, Mario Batali. Which I think looks good on a chef. I think I've changed less—enough less, anyway, that I think you recognized me shortly after I came to work for Jairus.

Interesting that we both changed our names to escape that terrible time.

Not a day has gone by since that day that I haven't thought about Daniel and hated myself.

You never heard the truth of what happened that evening. No one has. I couldn't say anything for fear I might end up dead too.

It was my fault that Daniel died.

I was on the phone with my boyfriend, Saul.

I had been a foolish seventeen-year-old girl who'd run away with an older guy who promised the world then gradually took away what little world I had. He was an abuser and by the time I came to work for you, when I was eighteen, I was totally captive to that weird codependent, love-hate relationship of the abused. Still telling myself that all I needed was to do better, be better, and Saul would turn nice and would love me.

We talked on the phone the whole time I was at your house with Daniel, every time I was there. Saul said that if I hung up that phone, he'd come over there and kill me. Kill us all, because he was certain that if I wasn't on that phone with him I was "banging" you.

I was on the phone that evening, as usual. I hadn't noticed Daniel had woken up and gotten off the little bed I always made up for him on the floor in the living room so I could watch him and the TV while I stayed on the phone with Saul. Saul had started yelling at me about some stupid little mistake I'd made. I was crying. Totally focused on what he was saying because he'd often ask me to repeat things he said to make sure I was listening to him.

It was when I had to go to the bathroom, taking the cordless phone with me of course, that I found Daniel. I could tell he was dead.

I screamed, but Saul told me I'd better shut up. He said he'd be there in ten minutes and that I'd better be right by the intercom to buzz him into the building when he got there or he'd beat me. He got there and ...

No. I can't write what he coldly did with his bare hands to your son. You know what the autopsy showed. That he'd landed on the brace of a chair that had back legs that extended out so that it was possible for Daniel to have lost his balance and fallen across the brace without hitting his head on the chair seat. That he'd landed with his throat across the brace and smashed his windpipe.

You know the chair they meant.

Saul told me everything to say to the police. Had me repeat it over and over, then he had me call 911.

This was what I told the paramedics when they questioned me:

I'd seen Daniel fall but there was nothing I could do, he was gasping. I tried to do the baby Heimlich maneuver and it hadn't done anything so I called 911. Then I had called my boyfriend to be with me because I was scared. He had arrived moments before they did.

Oh yes—Saul was there. With his arm around me like he was comforting me. They couldn't see that he was pinching the side of my left breast to make sure I said what he'd told me to say and nothing else.

It left yet another bruise on me courtesy of Saul.

They all said I wasn't at fault. Daniel was old enough to walk and run and no one watches a child absolutely every single moment.

I think what really happened was he'd choked on something he'd picked up off the floor.

I should have heard him. Would have heard him if I hadn't been on the phone with Saul.

Later, I became pregnant. Saul forced me to abort our child and then he beat me for having been so stupid as to put him through the hassle of dealing with making me do it.

The next day I limped my way to my old friend's house. She knew about one of those places that helps abused women escape and they took me away from there like I was a slave on the old underground railroad.

All new papers. All new me.

But I took a name that would help me remember who I was. My dad's mother's first and maiden name: Theresie Schmid.

I'll skip to when I came to the Twomblys'.

Jairus made it clear from the start that part of why he was hiring me was to test his wife. He said he'd got to the place where he wasn't sure she cared about him or their children, or if she just cared about her station in life as the wife of a rich and important man and the money she would get if he passed away before she did. He said he knew there hadn't been any affairs; he just wanted to know if she cared. If their relationship, and her relationship with the children, was threatened, how would she react.

At first, I'll admit, I wondered myself. So, I went further than Jairus had instructed me to. I doted on Madison and sent "care packages" to Jam VII. And yes, flirted with Jairus more than I should have. Then he told me to start planning events she'd always planned.

I could see her starting to crack. In mid December I told Jairus I should leave, but he seemed confused. Like he couldn't make the decision. He finally told me that there was too much going on over the holiday and it would look strange for him to let a PA go in the middle of it all. Wait until into January, he said.

I think it's gone on long enough.

Amy is starting to wake up to how good she has it. I think she'll be okay if I go. But she's on the knife's edge and I'm afraid she might completely lose it if I stay any longer. I'm going to quit Monday morning and leave right away.

And I'll be out of this—another bad situation that I shouldn't have let myself get into—and out of your sight as well.

I'm so sorry you've had to see me and be around me again.

I guess I haven't changed as much as I'd hoped.

Sally Bosch/Resie Schmid

Thank You

THANKS TO MY DEAR FAMILY: MY HUSBAND, OUR SON AND HIS family, our daughter and her family. They all have helped me to "Believe in the power of believing in myself." I love you all so much. And thank you to my extended family, who have joined along with them in helping me follow this dream.

Thank you to Mary Rosenblum who continues to encourage and support me as my writing coach, editor, and friend. I wouldn't make it through the process if it weren't for her. And thank you to my dear friend and beta-reader Vicki Biggerstaff, who catches the "boo-boos" that Mary and I miss.

Thank you to everyone on the Promontory Press team. Everyone has been patient and caring when dealing with this overly emotional author. I treasure you all.

Thank you to my many readers. Without you there would be no reason to write the *Emory Crawford Mysteries*. My hope is to give you a break from your everyday lives. To bring you some laughs, maybe some tears, and good clues to ponder. Thank you all for inviting everyone in Twombly to be a part of your lives.

Acknowledgements

FURLS FIBERARTS | AUSTIN, TX

furlscrochet.com

Many thanks to Harrison Richards, designer of the Furls crochet hooks and owner of the company, for giving me permission to use the company name, and the Bloodwood hook specifically, for this book. The hooks are beautiful and a joy to crochet with. My own size F Heirloom Bloodwood hook was used for the cover of *The Devil's Hook*.

P.D. LYLE, M.D. | LAKE FOREST, CA

dplylemd.com

Thanks also go to Dr. Lyle for answering my questions about where on the body a crochet hook with the specifications of the Furls Bloodwood hook could cause a fatal injury. Dr. Lyle has published numerous books to help authors with such questions, has written his own mystery novels and has consulted on several TV programs including *Law & Order*, *CSI: Miami*, *Cold Case*, and *House*.

PRAIRIE ROSE ALPACAS | PLEASANT PLAINS, IL

alpacafarms.iaoba.com/farm-alpacas/3913/prairie-rose-alpacas-llc

Thanks to Barb and Bruce Bernardi for permission to use the name of their wonderful alpaca farm here in central Illinois, helping me keep the regional flavor of the *Emory Crawford Mysteries* series.

About the Author

PEARL R. MEAKER IS AN UPPER-middle-aged, short, pudgy homemaker, mother, and grandmother who in 2002 decided to be a writer. She grew up in Dearborn, MI., and has lived most of her life in several states across the American Midwest. She and her husband like small-ish towns more than huge cities. Over the years she's worked different jobs in the various places she has lived, but always came back to being at home with her family. She excels in creative fields, such as writing, music, drama, and art, with hobbies including knitting, crochet, calligraphy, origami, needlepoint, embroidery, counted cross-stitch, very amateur bluegrass fiddling, and both foil and sabre fencing.